About the Author

Emma Timpany is an award-winning author of short story collections. Born and raised in Dunedin, New Zealand, Emma now lives in where she is married and has

Other books by the Author

Over the Dam

The Lost of Syros

*Cornish Short Stories: A Collection of
Contemporary Cornish Writing.* Co-editor.

Travelling in the Dark

EMMA TIMPANY

Fairlight Books

First published by Fairlight Books 2018

Fairlight Books
Summertown Pavilion,
18 - 24 Middle Way,
Oxford, OX2 7LG

A CIP catalogue record for this book is available from the British Library

1 2 3 4 5 6 7 8 9 10

ISBN 978-1-912054-48-0

www.fairlightbooks.com

Printed and bound in Great Britain by Clays Ltd, Elcograf S.p.A.

Designed by Sara Wood

Illustrated by Sam Kalda
www.folioart.co.uk

MIX
Paper from responsible sources
FSC® C018072

This book was written for my daughters, Iris and Lauren. It is dedicated to them and to Adam, who understands.

1

Sarah is on an aeroplane, crossing the night sky. Her hands are folded in her lap. Outside the window there is darkness. She could slide the small, white window blind down, close out the night, but somehow she cannot bring herself to make this one small act. The sense that she sometimes gets, that she must keep watching or she'll miss something of importance, is intense, though she cannot see anything beyond the veil of ice crystals. No stars, no satellites. No planets. No moon. No radiant light from some far city. For a moment, she turns away from the window and leans over the child sleeping beside her, gathering up a few scattered bricks of Lego before tucking a stray corner of blanket beneath his shoulder.

It is ten years since she has been on a long-haul flight; ten years since she was last at home. Some things are the same: the plastic smell of the plane's interior; the yeasty fug of bread rolls; the blurred aroma of food warming in stainless steel cabinets; the sickly sweet undertone of aviation fuel; the recycled air which dries her skin, her lips, the inside of her nose. Other things are different. The aeroplane, an Airbus, is larger and less noisy than the 747s she remembers. Sarah and the child were able to watch their take-off from a camera attached to its tailfin. The complimentary blankets – a tasteful charcoal colour – no longer make strands of her hair levitate with static; the pillows have mouse-grey covers of real cotton, smooth and cool to the touch.

On the tray in front of Sarah is a notebook, a useful size, not too bulky, small enough to fit comfortably into a handbag. On the white cover is a design, the golden curlicues of an elaborate crown and, underneath it, the words *Queen Of Everything*. When Sarah looks at it she sometimes wants to laugh, sometimes to cry, it is so far from the truth.

When her husband James decided to leave, Sarah saw a counsellor. At one of their sessions, the counsellor told Sarah that writing things down sometimes helps. Writing down anything that comes to mind, anyhow: in a notebook, on a scrap of paper, in sand. Memories, fragments, feelings. No matter how random, never mind how disjointed.

The child wakes and asks, 'Are we there yet?'

''Fraid not,' Sarah says. 'We still have a long way to go.'

She is watching a movie, set in Samoa. A man is cutting down taro plants with a machete. His house is settled among lush trees, its sides made of woven screens; there are bathing pools in the forest's dark.

8

Home. The movie is about a family of outcasts, but even they have a true home in their landscape.

Being on the plane is a kind of limbo; life yet not real life: meals on trays, entertainment on tap, unlike ground life with its routines, its night and day, its steady hours. Up here she is briefly free of those constraints, slipping across countries through the shimmering boundaries of time. Looking down from a height, her mind, for so long bogged down with legal intricacies, endless paperwork, is free to make out patterns usually hidden from her. When the movie finishes, she closes her eyes.

She wakes as the plane begins to make that odd noise, as if grating against the atmosphere, which means it is beginning its descent. Sarah had been dreaming a weird, disjointed aeroplane dream. She was once again in the garden of her childhood. Her father was there, nearby but just out of sight, digging the carrot-orange soil. She had been a child again, full of love for every flower, every living thing except perhaps the earwigs who seemed to be found in the heart of each geometric puzzle of a dahlia, each labyrinth of rose. Looking up she'd seen the sunlight glinting off the mud-dulled silver tines of his garden fork, his too-long hair touching his collar, the tufted wool of his jersey, pulled by rose thorns, rough as the outside of a fantail's nest. He was working the ground, preparing to plant a ring of rose bushes around the base of a cherry tree.

She wipes her eyes on a paper towel, afraid the child will notice, but he is engrossed in a brightly coloured cartoon, the only realm where the baddies always lose and the goodies always win.

They are in Singapore, at Changi Airport. The journey from England to New Zealand is so long that it is necessary to stop halfway for the plane to be cleaned and refuelled. The night air of the roof garden is warm, wet. In the centre of the garden, a fountain flows into itself. Sunken bulbs project pulses of rainbow onto the pale jets of water. The child rushes over and, plunging his hands into the streams, waves them, disrupting the performance. Around them, people sit on benches, smoking. Beside the benches are small, curved beds full of cactus-type plants, juicy-centred, covered in spikes. She warns the child not to go near them, not to be tempted to reach out with his fingers to touch them.

Back inside, Sarah walks up and down the long corridors, trying to get her circulation flowing while the child runs in loops around her.

'See these runways?' Sarah says.

'Yeah.'

'Your great-grandfather helped to build them.'

'Oh, really?' the child says. 'Did he do it all by himself?'

'No. He was a soldier. He was captured by the Japanese. During the Second World War. The prisoners were forced to build this airport.'

'*Pow! Pow, pow, pow!*' The child pretends to shoot the workers, clad in fluorescent vests, who move across the concrete, dwarfed by gantries and the dull silver bellies of the waiting aircraft.

Her grandfather was long dead, as was her father, Ross. And that was the root of the trouble, because he'd left a house to his children and cut his wife out. And he'd had Sarah and Nicki late. He was fifty when he died but they were still only children. Everything was to be kept in trust till they were eighteen – deemed officially of age – when her mother and sister forced Sarah to sign over a third of the house to her mother.

'It should have been hers all along,' her sister, Nicki, had said at the time, on her mother's side as always.

'And you'll get it back in the end,' Maria, their mother, reminded her.

The house in the mountains should have been a retirement home, but Sarah's father did not live long enough to retire. Beneath her ribs there was that ache, a kind of tugging in her chest that pulled and twisted until she felt that she could not bear it any longer.

It was around the age of eighteen, too, that Sarah had lost her grip on time. When she tries to think back, the years swirl and eddy coldly around her. Out-of-sequence memories pour past, like a jumble of cows and cars and crates riding a dark tide of flood-water. She is lying on a jetty, the heat from its wooden planks warming her back. She is standing on Patrick's leg as she climbs in through his window. Kitty is peeling an orange. Sarah is standing in the river, watching her father swim against the current. A chair is flying through the air towards her. And there, with Aunty Veronica, in a room with silver wallpaper, is someone whose face she cannot see.

2

Her parents had been back from Aunty Veronica's for a week, maybe two. Her mother was brushing Sarah's hair, and Sarah was crying because her hair was fine but very thick and the brush got tangled in it and then her mother tugged and the hair felt as though it was coming out in clumps.

'What's all the fuss about? I could hear you screaming out in the garden.'

Her father had come into the room. He smelt wrong. His eyes, when he looked at her, were cold.

'Her hair. It's too long,' her mother said. 'She hates having it brushed. I don't know what we're going to do when she starts school next week.'

'Must get it from your side of the family,' her father said. 'You'd better do something about it, Maria.'

Her mother did not take Sarah to the hairdresser's. She went with her Nana. When the long strands of her hair started tumbling to the floor, Nana put her hand on the hairdresser's arm and asked, 'What are you doing?'

'Her mother said to cut it really short, so it's easier for school.'

Nana said nothing. Everyone knew Ross hated short hair on girls.

'It does seem a bit harsh, doesn't it?' the hairdresser said.

Sarah's hair had always surrounded her. Now it was at most two inches long all over. Her real self was on the floor, being swept up and loaded into the dustbin. The face in the mirror was not hers. Even her eyes, a weird watery-blue, though her parents' and sister's eyes were brown, were someone else's too.

3

'Mummy. Mummy?' The child is tugging at her hand.

'What is it? Did I fall asleep?'

'No, but you weren't listening when I was talking to you.'

'Sorry. I wonder what the time is.' Sarah looks at her watch with pretend efficiency, not sure which time zone she is in, or what the local time should be, even approximately. She looks at the child, then, taking his hand, squeezes it.

Soon she'll see Patrick. It must be almost twenty years since they ran along the beach every school lunchtime. Should she call him?

'Let's see if we can find a clock, shall we?' Sarah says to the child.

When they find a clock, she works out the time difference between Singapore and New Zealand. It is too early to ring Patrick. Sarah does not want to wake him, or disturb his sleep.

An hour before the plane is due to take off again, Sarah and the child make their way to the departure gate. The gate is deserted; the blue, moulded plastic seats around them are empty. As they settle down to wait, an Indian woman with an ochre bindi pushes a cleaning trolley past them painfully slowly, as if she were pushing it not along the smooth, flat corridors, but endlessly uphill. She pauses nearby, cleaning what is already clean, each part of the gleaming airport, before rolling her trolley on towards the restrooms. Smartly dressed officials whizz past her on Segways. Sarah checks her and the child's passports, boarding cards and plane tickets over and over again. She empties her own and the child's pockets of everything and seals a tube of lip balm, a miniature toothpaste and her jar of moisturiser inside a clear plastic bag.

Back on the aeroplane, the child settles into his seat, gleefully pressing buttons. Something of Singapore's warm night air – sweet with frangipani and aviation fuel – lingers on her skin, beneath her clothes; it lies trapped between strands of the child's hair; it is almost the same as the night air that blows through the open doors of her Aunty Veronica's house on the top of the hill, in the tropical far north of New Zealand. As the plane takes off, Singapore dissolves to a cluster of lights in a slab of darkness and then it, too, is gone.

When the child needs to go to the toilet, Sarah reaches over and gently touches the shoulder of the lady in the aisle seat. After taking off her headphones, the woman stands to let them pass. On the way back, catching Sarah's eye as they settle back into their seats, the woman asks, 'Where are you going?'

'New Zealand.'

'Whereabouts?'

'The far south. The nearest airport still open is at Katipu. From there we're driving to Port Glass.'

'Still got a long way to go then, haven't you? I'm getting off in Auckland. To stay with my daughter.'

'Is it your first visit?'

'I've been six times before. Now I'm retired I can come over every year. Get away from the English winter. What about you?'

'I was born in Port Glass. Grew up there. But I've lived in England since my son was born.'

'So you're going home to see your family. I expect your mother loves this one.' She points to the child who, saucer-eyed watching *Puss in Boots*, ignores them.

Sarah makes a non-committal noise and turns back to the window.

'Wasn't it awful, about the earthquake?'

The woman's voice startles her, pushing a wide, white hole into her thoughts.

'Excuse me?'

'Right in the middle of that city. So many people killed and injured.'

'Yes...'

'Oh, I'm sorry, my dear. You've gone pale. I hope you didn't lose anyone?'

'I, I...'

'I didn't mean to upset you. I shouldn't have brought it up. My daughter always says I don't

17

know when to keep my big mouth shut.' Reaching across, the woman pats Sarah's hand. 'Forget I said anything.'

Although they have not yet served the food, there is something stuck in Sarah's throat. She takes a sip of water and tries to wash it away. The woman has put her headphones on, leaned back and closed her eyes.

4

They had been supposed to leave early, at the crack of dawn, to miss the worst of the heat, but after her mother opened the envelope, the shouting started and then Sarah's mother tore the letter up, even tore up the envelope without ripping off the stamp, an exotic American prize for their collections. A photo drifted to the floor; her father with a cowboy hat on his thinning, too-long hair, a sheriff's badge pinned to his roll neck jumper. It floated briefly like a leaf, coming to rest on the lino under the kitchen table where Sarah was pressed into a ball, hedge-hogging. Her two front teeth had not long fallen out, and with her tongue she probed the gap tentatively, the familiar fear circling within her that her teeth would never reappear – or worse, grow back as fangs. After the screaming came silence and then she heard her father calling, *Sarah!* in his last-chance voice, *Get in the car or else we'll leave you here.* She had learnt the hard way that this was not an idle threat.

The windows were rolled down and air blew in, cool and wild, blasting on their faces, messing up the hair now grown jerkily back to her shoulders. As soon as they were on the motorway, the air made that funny thumping noise and the windows had to be rolled up. They travelled for what felt like hours, the car getting hotter and hotter. Sarah stared at the bald patch on the back of her father's head, wishing it were a lid that, at her touch, might spring open and by some magic make everything all right again. Thoughts like that, impossible thoughts, kept the hunger at bay. A burning slice of sun fell across her leg and she lifted her thighs slowly, feeling the resistance of skin stuck to the seat's hot vinyl, and slid sideways a few inches. She looked across at Nicki and Nicki stuck out her tongue.

After a while the green hills dotted with occasional sheep turned into bare, rocky ranges with a green river snaking through them. Trees stood in rows alongside the road. Huge sprinklers arced above some of them, spraying the trees with rainbow water. Others were covered in green mesh.

'Do you want to stop and get some fruit?' her father asked her mother.

Her mother did not answer.

'Nectarines are cheap here. So are plums. Cherries. Other soft fruit too. Let's have a look, shall we?'

Her father pulled the car over, as if he'd heard some word of assent when actually there had been none. 'Coming out, girls?'

'Okay.'

'Maria? Are you coming?'

Their mother stared ahead, her jaw locked.

Inside the vast, corrugated iron shed an ashy, almost animal dark lay in wait for them, panting out air as warm-breathed as a fire-wind. Sarah swerved away from the stench of rotting fruit pulsing out from the entrance and dived into a pool of shade which ran like a black river alongside a row of netted trees. They had the same saw-like edges to their leaves as her father's favourite cherry tree. That tree got hard little rich red berries on it in the autumn, but you couldn't eat them unless you were a bird. Sarah tried to stick her fingers through the netting, but it was too dense. She looked around in the dust for a stone to kick.

'When we get to Orua, do you want me to be your friend? We could play together for the whole holiday.' Nicki had sidled up to her, her cherry-stained lips curved into a smile. 'Well, do you?'

For a moment, Sarah thought Nicki was going to pinch or kick her as usual, but Nicki just stood there with her hands on her hips. When they walked to school every morning, Nicki was supposed to look after her, but as soon as they were out of sight of the house, Nicki raced ahead. If Sarah got too close, Nicki would throw stones and scream at her to go away.

'I know so many great games. The ones I play with my friends. It'd be fun.'

'What about all the other times? You say you'll play with me and then you don't.'

'I'll tell Mum and Dad you've been mean to me.'

'All right then.' Maybe this time Nicki really meant it.

'There's just one thing you have to do. And then I'll be your friend forever.'

'Promise? Put your hands out so I can see you haven't got your fingers crossed.'

'Oh, for God's sake. What's wrong with you? Don't you trust me? Why would I lie to you? Okay, then. Cross my heart and hope to die. Etcetera. Etcetera.'

'What do I have to do?'

'Go over to Dad and ask him something. Just a teeny little question.'

'Ask him what?'

'It's nothing bad.'

'Are you sure?'

Nicki sighed. Her face took on a suffering aspect, like the saints' faces in that book of their mother's. 'Of course I'm sure. It's just asking a teeny question.'

'What's the question?'

'Ask Dad if he's a wanker.'

'Isn't that a rude word?'

'Don't be silly. Go on, Sarah. He won't mind. Off you go.'

5

Hours later, after a series of sickening lurches over the Southern Alps, the plane tilts to one side, and Sarah stares out at the long, familiar east coast of southern New Zealand. Dark lines of pine trees bisect the gold-brown plains; milky-blue rivers split, spread into intricate braiding patterns, touching then pulling apart, widening, branching as they near the sea. The sea is intensely turquoise, except at the outlets where the river waters, rich with sediment, billow smokily into the salt. The roads are black liquorice straps; irrigation systems glint, casting water-strings which shatter into droplets as they fall.

A spine of mountains. Green-black beech climbing flanks, furring gullies. The snow fields that peculiar unearthly white, except where rock falls track across their faces like trails of dirty tears. Among the peaks, tarns shine in high, lost basins. The few clouds in the sky look unconvincing, barely there, a few wisps of vapour that might at any moment fall to pieces, merge into the blue. There's something dense, tooth-like, almost, about the peaks. A gap opens in them and Sarah finds herself nudging her son, pointing out a blue S-shape, jaggedy-edged as a lightning bolt drawn by a child.

'What is it?' the child says.

'That's Lake Katipu. And that…' she points to what looks like a thin tail wiggling off the side of the lake '… is the Findings River.'

The plane makes its way downwards. By the airport is a new roundabout and, to one side of it, a complex containing a petrol station and shopping centre. As they touch down, the plane slows so quickly they are thrown forwards in their seats.

Unimpressed by the heart-stopping scenery, the child shouts, 'Swimming pool. I saw a swimming pool. Lots of swimming pools!'

Sarah laughs. His hand, when she squeezes it, is damp with excitement.

'Have we got a swimming pool where we're staying?' the child says.

'There's one at the motel.'

'Great. Can I go for a swim? As soon as we get off the plane?'

'We have to collect our bags. Pick the hire car up. We could swim in the lake if you like.'

'I want to swim in the pool.'

'Okay. If you're not too tired. I don't see why not.'

'Woo-hoo!'

As they walk from the aeroplane to the baggage collection area, the sky above their heads is wide, violently blue; the surrounding air is thick with the rose-sweet smells of summer, tangs of sheep dirt, herb-scented dust carried on dry blasts of wind. At the edge of a lawn too green not to be irrigated, the child pauses. In front of them are hoardings showing pictures of the post-cataclysm city further north of here: piles of bricks and boards, fallen masonry, a shattered church spire.

'What happened to the buildings?' the child asks.

'They got broken.' The dust is burning her eyes. 'Because of the earthquake.'

'It looks like a giant stepped on them.'

'Yes,' Sarah says. 'Yes, it does.'

As they are about to enter the terminal, the child stops so suddenly she almost trips over him. He points to some sheer rock faces, riddled with fissures. 'Those mountains are weird.'

'They're a bit spooky, aren't they? But what do you think of the rest of the place? Do you like it?'

'It's sunny. It smells nice.'

Wild thyme and lake water and still a breath of snow and ice even in the summer air. 'They found gold here, lots of gold, in the river we saw from the aeroplane. That's why this town exists. That's why some of my family used to live here.'

'Gold like your ring?' The child's fingers stray to Sarah's wedding band, trying to wriggle it over her knuckle.

'Don't take it off. It might get lost.'

'Gold comes from rivers?'

'From the ground. Usually you have to dig for it. Here, the water washed it loose from the ground and the rocks. So it was quite easy to get hold of it, to pan or dredge it out.'

'Why haven't you got a ring with a stone in?'

'Wedding rings don't usually have stones in them. Engagement rings do.'

'Why haven't you got an engagement ring?'

'Dad and I got married when we were very young. Dad couldn't afford to buy me one.'

'Why did you and Dad split up again?'

'You know why. I've told you lots of times. Daddy found another lady and fell in love with her. And now they're married to each other. And they've got the new baby and all her other children to look after so that keeps them very, very busy. But Daddy still loves you very, very much.'

'Why do you still wear it?'

'This isn't the ring that Daddy gave me. When we stopped being married I gave it back to him.' A lie. The truth was, in a fit of rage, she had flushed her wedding band down the toilet. 'This ring belonged to my great-grandmother. It's very old. The gold comes from the river that we saw. On the aeroplane. Remember?'

Inside, now, Sarah sees their suitcases stutter past and pulls them from the conveyer belt.

'Please can I put it on?' the child says.

'Okay, but only for a moment.'

Sarah slips the ring onto his finger and then they walk towards the bright rectangle of light outside the foyer doors.

6

Twenty minutes later, as they crossed the pass and descended into a valley, boxes of over-ripe fruit jammed into the footwells, her mother said, 'For God's sake, Sarah, would you stop that snivelling. Blow your nose.' It was the first time Maria had spoken in hours.

Sarah's backside and the backs of her knees were still smarting from where her father had whacked her, one... two... three... four... five times with his hand, and six... seven... eight... nine... ten times with his bunch of keys. She had told him that Nicki had told her to say it, but he didn't seem to hear her. On the way back to the car, Nicki had grabbed her arm and, squeezing it too tightly, whispered, 'I can't believe you actually asked him. I can't believe you fell for it. But then you always do, don't you? You never learn, do you? It's so funny. You are so unbelievably stupid. Why would I ever, ever want to play with a retard like you?'

Outside the window, the tussock rippled gold and then white under the wind's tongue. A funny smell, dry and powdery; dusty, stubby plants. In the shade of the pines, two magpies pecked cones. And, just as her eyes were closing and she was happily escaping into the world of dreams, the car turned off the road and their father said, 'We're here.'

The ground rose into a wave of earth. Following her father from the car, Sarah put out her arms and entered a world of wildflowers, walking further and further until she was nose-deep in them. Some were tall with soft grey leaves, like lamb's lug, and buttery yellow flowers. Others were tall and spiky, a purple kind of blue. Here the dandelions grew tall and fine, unlike their squat cousins on the lawn at home. But soon this would be home as well, her father was saying, a holiday home, a retirement home, because he was getting old and tired; this would be a place for him to come and rest.

In the middle of the field of flowers he stopped and pulled a roll of paper from his pocket, thin pale paper, turned and began to measure out the invisible rooms of the ghost house drawn on it in long, loose strides.

From behind her, Sarah heard the sound of the car starting.

'Where's Mum going?' Nicki said.

Nicki still stood on the edge of the white dust road, her hands balled into fists. Their father had his back to them, but he must have heard the engine start, even if he didn't see their mother drive off. It happened quite often at home, but it never lost a certain startling quality, the noise of their mother slamming the car door and roaring off, after reversing with reckless haste up the drive. They looked at their father, absorbed in crushing the wildflowers into lines representing the rooms-to-be.

Nicki sat down and idly ripped the heads off a stand of creamy clover.

The hot blows of a new kind of sun fell on Sarah's skin. There were no clouds here like there were on the coast, no green-black stands of bush that she could see. The hills were bare and brown as summer limbs yet, further off, between their peaks, the mountains held baskets of pure white snow up to the sky. Even though it was so far away, she could smell the snow, a funny kind of cold, clean smell. Under the heat of this sun, how did the snow not melt? The air over the mountains was filled with a kind of shimmer, as if large, barely visible beings were moving over the tops, and sometimes the surface of the lake gave a little shiver as if one of the huge beings had dipped a toe into the water. The new house place was strange; her throat was dusty, her senses dulled with sun.

When her father finished flattening the flowers and called, 'Come on!' she and Nicki leapt across the meadow towards him, onto the white dust road, towards the shadow of the pines.

'Woah.'

Because Sarah had been trailing behind, chewing a hank of hair, kicking drifts of white dust, dropping pine cones in the deep, clear-watered stream, Nicki was the first to reach the playground, immediately peeling off towards the swings and demanding to be pushed faster-faster-higher-higher. There were monkey bars and a four-square court and an enormous pink concrete elephant; its tail turned out to be the steps, its trunk the slide.

'Go on. Off you go and play.' Their father gave Nicki one final shove on the swing and then he turned and began to walk towards the lakeshore. Sarah watched as he dawdled a little to and fro, followed by a posse of disappointed ducks, before bending awkwardly to find flat stones to skim on the dead calm water. From the top of the elephant slide, Sarah looked over at him and waved hugely, but he did not see her. He turned, though, when, after a little while, the car pulled up and their mother walked across the shore towards him. He held her in his arms while she rubbed her face back and forth across the front of his shirt.

'Get a move on!' Nicki kicked her in the small of her back and Sarah shot forwards, rushing down the long silver tongue of the slide and landing with a painful bump in a patch of cone-littered gravel. 'Oh, for God's sake. Why are you crying? You're such a little cry baby. Boo hoo. Gonna run off and tell Mummy and Daddy?'

Nicki's fingers were small and bone-fine. You wouldn't think that there was enough strength in them to give such a powerful twisting pinch.

'Well, let me tell you something, little miss cry baby.' Nicki pressed her face down close to Sarah's.

'Even if you do tell them, they won't care. I heard them talking. They don't love you. They only love me. You're a freak. Nobody likes you. Nobody wants you. It's about time you got some facts into that derr-brain of yours.'

Run, run as fast as you can. Out of the sun, into the shade of some funny trees which stood on the shore, their leaves falling and swaying like hair. Her father called them weeping something, but what exactly Sarah had forgotten.

7

There is no view of the lake from their room because the motel they are staying in was built facing the wrong way round. Somehow, the builders got the plans back to front. Instead of looking towards the mountains and the lake, the room faces the golden plains of grassland that run down to the Findings River. Sarah does not mind this, and the child does not notice. Twenty, or perhaps thirty, years ago, it had been a great scandal, but now most people had stopped caring, or had forgotten about it, if they had ever known.

Sarah opens the sliding door and steps out onto the balcony. Though now in shade, the concrete is warm beneath her feet, as is the breeze rising up the hillside. The ring is tight on her finger; her hands and feet feel swollen from the combination of the flight and sudden heat.

'May I get all my Lego out?' The child is behind her, tapping on her hip.

'Do you want to do it now? I thought you wanted to go for a swim?'

'I want to get it ready, so I can play with it later.'

Leaving the door open, Sarah hauls the suitcase onto the bed and rummages through the clothes until she feels the large bag of Lego the child has insisted on bringing. She is surprised to find that his towers and buildings, ramps and other constructions have survived the journey fairly intact. The child immediately claims an area around a small desk, integrating the desk and chair legs into his design. Sarah pulls their swimming togs out of the jumble, and then sits on the edge of the bed, rubbing at her ankles.

After getting changed, they go out to the pool. As Sarah lowers herself into the water, the bodily sensation of pressure from hurtling through the sky for all those hours immediately eases. She tips her head back, floats; her bones, now water-light, feel as if they have become as hollow as a bird's. At the far end of the pool she rights herself, elbows folded on the edge to anchor her.

There is a fine view of the lake and mountains. The child ignores it, absorbed in fishing for pool toys, diving down to fetch them from the shiny blue tiles over and over again. Sleek-bodied, arms extended, he presses his palms together into a beak that breaks the surface of the water. With his bronzy hair and turquoise and navy trunks and swim vest he looks just like a kingfisher. Watching him, she tries to remember what it was like, being lost in the happy repetitiveness of childhood. The child's absorption reminds her of Patrick, who was never more content than when he was working on his tennis serve, perfecting his batting or bowling skills, shooting hoops, or throwing himself recklessly across a goal mouth, brim-full of the belief that he could save every shot.

'Are you enjoying yourself?' Sarah asks.

'This is great. How long are we staying here for?'

'We're heading south tomorrow.'

'Why do we have to leave?'

'Because we're going to see Patrick.'

'Has he got a swimming pool?'

'I'm not entirely sure, but I don't think so.'

'Why are we going to see him?'

'He's Mummy's friend. Things have been hard for him lately. So we're going to visit him.'

'How will that help?'

The truth is, she doesn't know. After a while she says, simply, 'It's what friends do.'

'You must really like him.'

'Yes,' Sarah says. 'I do.' Though it hasn't always been the case. There have been times when she's come close to hating him, too.

The minutes burn away. She watches the water ripple on the surface of the pool; many colours dart across it, fleetingly: silver, navy, a pinkish-yellow. Sharp-edged memories crowd around her, poke into her, all elbows and knees. She closes her eyes; the light burns pink through the thin skin of her eyelids. Patrick, the young, sporty Patrick, and the Patrick who waits for her now, fade into the dazzle.

A man limps over to the side of the pool. Though he looks nothing like her father, that is who he reminds her of because he walks like a man in pain.

The sun is beginning to burn Sarah's winter-pale skin in spite of the sun cream she has put on. The child is arcing under the water. When he breaks the surface, she says, 'Time to go inside.'

'Aww.'

'We can swim again later.'

As Sarah and the child walk back into the motel, they pause in the foyer for a second or two, waiting for their eyes to adjust to the dimness within. For a moment, the ground is tilting, buckling, and then everything begins to shudder. She puts her hand out and touches the wall, drawing the child close, and then the sensation passes as swiftly and subtly as it came. Beneath the pads of her fingers, the paint is chalky. The wall is the dim, musky pink of a type of sweet she liked as a child; for a moment, she can taste again a dry burst of powdered sugar, grainy in her mouth.

'Ow. Too tight.' The child wriggles, shaking his body free of hers.

'Sorry. I didn't mean to... Are you okay?'

'You did it too hard.' He stamps on her foot.

'Don't shout. You didn't..? Did you just... feel anything?'

'Like what?'

'Like... it doesn't matter.' It is true she is tired. They have been travelling non-stop for two days.

She looks down at the child and smiles at him with what she hopes is reassurance and, as they cross to the elevator, she notes their relative position to exits and windows, doorways and nearby desks or tables that they might seek shelter under.

'Are you all right, Mum?' the child says.

'Got the wobbles for a moment. Jetlag, probably. I think I need to put my feet up for a minute.'

Between the hours of 11 a.m. and 3 p.m. the fair-skinned, like Sarah and the child, are advised to take cover from the sun. So it is a toss-up. There are six thousand seismic events a year in New Zealand, many of them too small to feel. If a quake is coming, it is safer outside. In and of themselves, earthquakes do not necessarily kill people. Falling buildings kill people. People escaping from falling buildings rush straight into the middle of busy roads.

'Who did this?' The child howls, running to the centre of the room, hands in hair.

'What's the matter?'

'Someone knocked my city over.'

His multi-coloured Lego tower has toppled side-ways; his playground slide and climbing frame have overbalanced; the ramp carefully propped against the footrest of the desk lies flat on the floor.

So it wasn't her imagination playing tricks on her. 'Oh dear,' Sarah says. 'Shall I help you fix it?'

The child sighs as deeply as a disillusioned adult, but he shakes his head. 'You wouldn't do it right.' A pause. 'No offence.'

Suddenly tired, Sarah moves from the armchair to the bed. The child, his restoration complete, pulls out the plastic bag full of spare bricks and scatters them on the floor. He loves building: out of the same few hundred pieces he constructs castles, playgrounds, houses, schools. Sometimes he sketches out designs and then attempts to create them, as if he were training himself for a future career in architecture. Lying back, she can hear the gentle clicking sounds as he fuses the blocks together.

'What are you making this time?' Sarah folds her hands across her stomach and lets her eyes close.

'Guess.'

'An airport?'

'No. Guess again.'

'A school?'

'No. Guess again.' He gives a little chuckle. 'Actually, you'll never guess.'

'Actually, you're probably right. So you had better tell me.'

'No!'

'Go on. Please?'

'A swimming pool.'

8

Aunty Veronica's house was on the top of the hill. Sarah, Nicki and their cousins were in the indoor swimming pool and Jem was there, too. Sarah was seven. She had never met Jem before, even though he was some sort of relative. He had black hair on his head and chest and arms and legs. His eyes were a strange light blue. When he talked to Sarah, he stood with his feet apart and put his hands on his hips. 'So. You're Maria's daughter, are you?'

Within minutes he had Veronica's children at each other's throats. Then he told them not to bother going down the slide into the pool but to queue up on the balcony and then climb up onto the railing and jump straight into the water. He lined them up. It was almost Sarah's turn. As Jem's hand slapped between her cousin's shoulder blades, launching him into space, Sarah swivelled on one wet foot and ran, heart bursting, sometimes skidding on the marble tiles so that she almost fell, through room after room after room. There, in the shade of the terrace – there they were.

'Mum!'

Seeing Sarah was dripping wet, Maria pushed her away. 'Sarah? Why aren't you in the pool? What's wrong?'

Her mother's mouth was puckered, her eyebrows lowered as if she were angry. Sarah shrugged, looked down at the marble tiles, held her tummy.

'Do you need the toilet?' Maria asked.

'My tummy feels funny.'

'Swimming can make you hungry.' Drips of condensation fell from Veronica's glass onto her skirt.

'I'm hungry.' I don't like that man.

'What's Jem up to in there? Aren't you having fun?'

I hate him. He's mean. You can tell he's mean. Sarah's stomach lurched. She shrugged.

'Remember the fun we had,' Veronica said, raising the triangle glass to her lips and sipping. 'We all used to go out together. Remember, Maria?'

'I'm hardly likely to forget.' Maria gave a small, high laugh.

'Can you guess who Jem used to be in love with, Sarah?' Veronica leaned forwards.

'That's enough, Veronica.' Maria's smile disappeared. 'Off you go now, Sarah. Go and play.'

9

Sarah opens her eyes. Her heart is pounding too loud, too fast. The blade-like edge of fear, slicing through her dream, waking her, has left her throat dry, constricting the soft lining, robbing it of moisture. The ceiling ripples with glyphs of light beamed on to it by the dangling crystals of a modern, minimalist chandelier. One hand presses on the soft cotton bedspread; the other, trapped beneath her body, is numb. It flops onto the cover, spiked by pins and needles as it returns to life. As she reaches over for the glass of water on the bedside table, she sees him. She is not alone. There on the floor, humming to himself, is her child. At the time, it seemed his baby years would last forever. But he is a baby no more. He is an eight-year-old boy who loves building, who loves swimming pools and movies and Lego. When he's absorbed in his play like this, she doesn't want to disturb him. But she doesn't want to stay in the motel room either. The air is stuffy, synthetic, unhealthy, as if it has been tainted by a host of her memories which hold a greater terror for her than any of her nightmares.

'What say we go to the lake?' she says, righting herself. 'We could get some fish and chips for dinner and eat them on the shore.'

'Okay.'

After parking on a suburban street, they walk lakeward, a steaming, newspaper-wrapped bundle tucked under Sarah's arm. Inside the houses they pass, inside rooms, the blue dance of screens. No picnicking families are spread out under the shade of the weeping willows; no toddlers fill pails with stones. At 6 p.m. Sarah and the child have the entire shore, mile after mile of it, to themselves.

Salty chips; flaky fish inside crisp, beery batter. A swig from a bottle of water, unpleasantly tepid from time spent in the hot interior of the hire car. After Sarah and the child have eaten, they walk across the pebbles to the water and wash the greasy, grainy residue from their fingers and mouths. The surface of the lake is calm. No boats pass; the only noise is the dim, oceanic roar of traffic from the lakeside road.

Sarah wanders along the water's edge, rolling her shoulders, swinging her arms. The child piles up rocks, skims stones; he runs back and forth between the weeping willows, parting their branches like hair, climbing their bending trunks. Sarah goes back and settles where she's left her bag, swatting a sandfly which lands among the tiny dark moles scattered over her skin. Eventually, slowing, weighed down by supper, the child comes over and sits beside her, nudging her arm with lamb-like persistence until she drapes it over his shoulder.

If she asks the child whether he's tired and ready to go, he'll say 'No', so she says, 'Shall I tell you a story?'

It is almost seven o'clock. Even the traffic is quietening down and everything – trees, mountains, lake, stones, sky – has started to dissolve, to become one in a world awash with deep, sleepy blues.

'What's the story about?' A juddering stretch, then a half yawn, as he snuggles deeper into her side.

'A demon, a princess, a young man, and a lake that rises and falls mysteriously...'

'Is it true?'

'Sort of. But not really.'

'Go ahead.'

'Remember those jaggedy wild mountains you noticed earlier?' Sarah points across the lake. 'A long time ago a demon called a "tipua" lived up there. He was always making life difficult for the people who lived on the lakeshore, stealing their food and sometimes, when he was *really* hungry, catching and eating them. But one day he grabbed a girl who was so beautiful that the tipua fell in love with her. Instead of eating her, he took her back to his mountain lair and tied her up with magical dog-skin ropes. A young man of the tribe also loved the girl and

43

decided he must rescue her. The young man knew that when the warm north-westerly wind blows, the tipua has to sleep. So when he felt the warm wind on his face, the young man headed for the mountains and found the tipua lying on his side, dead to the world, snoring so loudly that the ground all around shook. But when the young man tried to rescue the girl, he found he could not untie the magical ropes, nor could he cut them. When she realised this, the girl began to cry. Her tears melted the ropes, and she was free.'

'But what about when the tipua woke up? He must've been really mad. I bet he ate both of them, didn't he?'

'The young man was clever, like you, and he thought exactly the same thing. So while the demon was still sleeping, the young man piled brushwood around the tipua's body and set light to it. In his agony, the tipua drew his knees up to his chest. His body sank deeper and deeper into the valley, forming the lake. Only his great heart was not consumed in the fire. They say it beats still, in the very bottom of the lake. If you watch carefully, you'll see that the water level goes up and down and waves rise out of nowhere.'

'Really?'

'Yes. Perhaps we'll be lucky enough to see it. Shall we watch?'

'Okay.'

'Watch.'

'I can't see anything.'

'Watch. That's it. Watch the water. Keep watching. Now, look, it's happening now.'

Tugging Sarah along with him, the child runs to the water's edge. The surface of the lake lifts and then, as if letting out a long-held breath, pushes a small series of waves across the stones, washing over their toes, lapping the shore.

'Was that a good story?'

'Yes. It was very good. But Mum...'

'Yes?'

'I feel a bit sorry for the tipua.'

'Me too. But what you've got to remember when you feel like that is that he used to eat lots of people, which isn't very nice, is it?' For a moment, they watch the waves in silence. 'And there's something else.'

'What?'

'Did I tell you that this lake is so deep that in some places they haven't found the bottom of it?'

'No.'

'Well, then. That's something else you need to know.' After brushing the top of his hair with her hand, Sarah kisses the child's cheek. 'Want to have a paddle before bed?'

No one's really sure why the lake level rises and falls. Geothermals, possibly. Atmospheric pressure, perhaps. Or a standing wave. The fire, the heat, comes from deep beneath the earth, in ways that are still not fully understood, a force unimaginably far from what can be seen on the lake's surface. But before these theories, the only explanation was that a great heart lay hidden in its depths, the heart of a demon destroyed by love.

10

Sarah had only been at her new school for a few weeks when this boy in her class, Patrick, had challenged her to a tennis match. She'd seen him watching her sometimes in the playground after school, hitting shot after shot against the backboard. Patrick was good at every sport they played, and they played the lot – cricket, tennis, basketball, volleyball, netball, soccer. Only co-ed rugby was banned for fear of injury. When everyone gathered round to watch, she could feel her face begin to burn, but once the game started she got her focus and felt the clarity – a cool, almost icy feeling – start.

Patrick was a good player but too impatient, fuming if she hit back a serve or shot he'd expected to be a winner. As the last ball hit the line, Sarah threw up her arms and shouted. Her shot was in. She'd beaten him, after the longest game of tennis ever. But now he was rushing towards her, letting his racquet drop from his hand and balling his fists as if she had done something wrong, and then he was pushing her back into the diamond-shaped wire fence around the court and saying, 'Think you're clever? Well, you were just lucky. I'll beat you next time.'

'There won't be a next time,' Sarah said and stamped on his foot.

The bell for the start of afternoon classes started ringing and she left him there, alone on the court, hopping on one leg.

A couple of weeks later, everyone had forgotten about tennis and running was the new thing. They did cross-country in winter and athletics in the summer, but now the head master decided they all need to run for twelve minutes every day, too. So, before lunch they changed into shorts and headed out down the long, straight road by the school, crossing over near the rugby ground and the playground with the concrete whale in it until they reached the sand dunes. Then it was up and over and along the beach, looping back by another lupin-lined path through dunes near the headland and coming out opposite the school.

Since the tennis match, Patrick hadn't spoken to her. This didn't surprise her as he'd never said anything to her up till the moment he'd challenged her to that game. But now, as they laced up their running shoes, she saw him looking at her, and then he nodded and they set off together. He was good at running and his legs were longer than hers, so Sarah struggled to keep pace with him, her heart pounding painfully against her ribs. On the beach, her feet sank in the dunes and cool, fine grains of sand poured into her shoes around her ankles, filling the empty space between insole and arch.

11

Next morning when Sarah wakes, she has only one thing on her mind. Patrick. So vivid is his presence, she feels as if she could touch him.

In part she is dreading seeing Patrick for the first time in years; in part she cannot wait to look upon his face. There have been times when she's felt that she might never see him again. It has been so long, more years than she wants to remember: much has happened to them both. *Perhaps*, she thinks, *Patrick will have changed. Perhaps we won't get on anymore.*

Over the lake the sky is coral and turquoise, the mountains black, as yet untouched by sun. But by the time they leave town, crossing over the Findings River, the sky is the whitish blue that spells another hot, cloudless day.

After following the contours of the river valley for an hour or so, they arrive where vast forests edge another lake, rising up to cover all but the summits of mountain after mountain. No one lives in the forests or the mountains; on the other side of all this wilderness are fiords and then the sea. In this temperate rainforest, it rains day after day, sometimes week after week. The rain is the same as the rain in her dreams: heavy, steady, an enclosing veil beyond which she cannot see.

But the fears of yesterday have loosened their grip on her. All is calm, peaceful. The sun shines, turning the surface of the water a smooth, glassy black.

'Ready for a break?' she asks. 'We could stop here for a quick walk. Have some lunch.'

In the rear-view mirror, the child's reflection raises and drops its shoulders. It's hard to know what he makes of it all. He seems to carry his whole world with him. At times it seems to encase him, as if childhood is a shell he can, at will, retreat into entirely. It almost makes her envious that, at any given point, only part of him ever emerges to engage with his surroundings. Since James left and, soon after, she lost the house in Orua, she's felt raw, as if she's been forced to shed her old, familiar skin but hasn't yet had time to grow a new one.

After parking by the shore, Sarah and the child walk to the end of the village, passing hunks of driftwood, whitened by their journey through the water. There is an aviary filled with native birds, their green and blue feathers perfect camouflage for the shadows beneath the bush, aside from the odd betraying flash of red beak, orange leg. A dam spans the outlet, a gap that seems ridiculously narrow compared with the vast acreage of water stretching for miles behind it. They climb metal stairs and cross a catwalk above foaming water, blackish green with decayed leaves.

The child, instead of running ahead, stays near, gripping her hand, mesmerised almost by the dizzying, roaring tumble beneath his feet. As they step off the bridge, the child looks at his damp legs and says, 'It was like an upside-down shower.'

They leave the thundering water behind and step into the cool breath of tree ferns, southern beech, kahikatea, following a springy brown path which winds gently away through the trees. Tomtits. Riflemen. Fantails. The fantails fly just in front of them and just behind, a stutter of feathers at the corner of their eyes, darting and swivelling, snaffling microscopic bugs disturbed by their passing feet.

'Look.' The child runs ahead, stooping to pick up something she cannot see from the path. He turns, holding a nest made of soft twigs and old silver-grey cobwebs, moss and lichen, rough on the outside but smooth and flawless within. It is empty, of course, its purpose past.

'What kind of bird makes this, Mum?'

'Might be a fantail's.' Sarah tries to think back to her years of biology lessons, the field trips into forests just like these. The outside of the nest is the grey-green of her father's old gardening jumper, similarly scattered with twigs. An image comes to mind, from a book cover, of a fantail sitting on a long, tapering nest, almost the shape of an inverted tear-drop. 'I think it probably is. Probably, almost definitely.'

'How do they make their nests?' The child turns it in his hands, eyes narrowed in examination.

'The birds collect things from the forest and then they weave them together.'

'How?'

'With their beaks.'

'Oh. Can we keep it?'

'We can keep it with us while we're travelling. But I don't think we'll be able to take it back to England.'

'Why not? I could have it in my room. In my cabinet. With my fossils and my rocks.'

'We'll see.'

'That means no. It's not fair. I hate this place.'

'You don't mean that.'

'Yes, I do. I don't see why we have to be here, going on a stupid walk.'

'I thought you'd like it.'

'Well, I don't. It's boring.'

What reason is there for him to love it as she does? He loves Lego and swimming pools, eating ice cream and watching movies. 'Would a polo mint help at all?'

'Two polo mints?'

'Okay.'

After wiping the tears off his cheeks, the child walks on, the nest cradled between his hands. She walks in silence beside him, hoping the soothing presence of the trees, the stillness and intoxicatingly pure air will calm him.

'Why do you like this forest, Mummy?' he asks, eventually.

'Because I came here once when I was a girl.'

'Did you use to like the fantails when you were little?'

'I used to love the fantails. I still do.' She shows the child how to hold his finger out and call to the birds by pressing his lips together to make a rapid kissing sound. 'One landed on my finger once. It felt so light.'

'I wish one would land on my finger.'

'I'm sure one will one day. I know a good story about a fantail.'

'Will you tell me?'

'Yes. But not now. Another time.'

'But you'll tell me later? Tonight. Promise?'

'Promise.'

'You won't forget, will you?'

'No. I promise.'

By the time they leave the trees, it is after midday. The child still refusing to be parted from it, she places the fantail's nest into the glovebox of the hired car. They buy sandwiches from a bakery and eat them on the shore. The child skims stones, watching them skip across the surprisingly strong skin that separates the world beneath the lake water from theirs.

They haven't walked particularly far, or at least it seemed not far to her, so Sarah is surprised that the child falls asleep as she drives to the southern end of the lake and out of the village. It must be a deep slumber because the rumblings she hears echoing off the rock faces do not wake him.

As they round the next corner, Sarah sees the road ahead has a line of traffic cones stretched across it. She indicates though no one is behind her, following a yellow road sign which reads 'Diversion' down an unsealed road to the left.

After a few kilometres of bumping along the corrugated surface, a film of dust has worked its way inside the car, settling on the dashboard. The child wakes up, groans quietly, and says, 'Are we not there yet? How much longer?'

At the end of the road, she pauses for longer than necessary, looking at the sign. To the right, the town of Makata, which she knows is a dead end. To the left, four little letters which might as well be made of razor blades. ORUA.

Not Orua. Anywhere but Orua. Even though she knows the answer to the question, Sarah presses her head against the steering wheel and whispers, 'Isn't there another road that we could take?'

12

'These are my nieces. They're visiting from down south. Port Glass. You know it? So cold down there,' Veronica told the waiter. 'I'm an alcoholic, so I don't drink anymore, but I'm sure the girls would like something, wouldn't you, girls?' Although it was barely midday, Veronica ordered her nieces, aged twelve and fourteen, a dry martini each. The waiter did not think to ask how old they were.

In Sarah's memory, Veronica had been deeply tanned and thin. Now she was much larger, her taut skin as shiny and brown as gravy. She wore a strapless sundress which should have flowed but instead made everything worse. The restaurant was in a newly opened shopping mall and the lighting was dim, though the wallpaper, an extraordinary silver colour, caught what little light there was and scattered it. Little patches of brightness glowed on the ceiling, on the plates and glasses and tablecloth, on their hair and clothes and skin.

When the martinis arrived, Veronica grabbed the cocktail sticks out of them. 'I never drink. I only eat the olives.' Veronica put her hand on the waiter's arm. 'It's okay to eat the olives. It isn't drinking to eat the olives.' After she had swallowed them, her eyes grew as hard as a shark's.

'That green suits you.' Veronica eyed Sarah's new dress.

Nicki drank some martini and said, 'Your earrings would go well with it, Aunty Veronica.'

'Yes, they would.' Yanking them from her ears, Veronica thrust them towards Sarah. 'Why don't you put them on?'

'No, thank you, they're very nice but...' Sarah kicked Nicki hard under the chair.

'Put them on. They match your dress; they match your eyes too. Put them on.' Veronica had this way of speaking very quietly that was somehow worse than shouting.

The earrings were made of paua, curving discs of shell rippling with rainbow light, clip-on, of course, because if God wanted us to have holes in our ears we would have been born with them. The clips dug into Sarah's lobes until they, too, began to burn as her face burned with the alcohol. Until now, until this very moment, she had loved paua shell. Although Sarah and Nicki had barely touched their drinks, Veronica ordered them another one each.

Veronica snapped the four empty toothpicks in half and dropped them on the side of her plate. The door to the restaurant opened, and she stood and began to wave at the man who had entered. Sarah felt her stomach curl; it looked like that strange man Veronica was always talking about.

'Look, girls. Look who it is.'

'Who cares?' Nicki snarled.

'Oh, my goodness!' Veronica said. 'Jem! What are you doing here?'

'Oh, you know. Out for a wander and some light refreshment. And then I noticed you lovely ladies hiding away in the corner.'

'Come and join us. Quick. Pull up a seat.'

'How old are you girls now?' Jem hung his pale blue jacket over the chair-back.

'I'm fourteen.' Nicki pointed to Sarah. 'And she's twelve.'

The new clothes Sarah was wearing scratched against her skin. Nicki wore her favourite T-shirt; on it was a picture of a black-gloved hand, sprinkled with diamanté, and 'BEAT IT' printed on a slant across the front.

'You're starting to look like your mother.' He nodded to Sarah. 'But you, Nicki, are just like your father.'

'Everyone says that,' Nicki muttered, flicking her eyes at him, her usual response when adults bored her. If she had been a cat, her tail would have started to twitch. 'Can't you think of anything original to say?'

'You're a feisty one, aren't you? I'll do my best to think of something *original*, as you put it. But first, tell me something. Why isn't your mother here with you?'

'She couldn't get away from work.' Nicki rubbed the pad of her thumb over the cream cushion of a chin zit. At the last moment, Maria had changed her mind about coming, sending them on the plane instead as unaccompanied minors, luggage labels attached to their clothes as if they were pieces of baggage.

'I see.'

The waiter came over to take their food orders, but Jem, saying he wasn't hungry, only ordered a carafe of red wine. After the waiter left, Veronica seemed agitated. Saying she was going to check their orders, she went over to the bar. Though her back was to them, Sarah could see her reflection in a mirror, pointing at bottles.

'Let me see. Something original. Shall I tell you a story while your aunt is otherwise engaged?'

Sarah looked at Nicki. She nodded. They both assumed it would be about their parents. All the grown-ups they knew liked telling them stories about their parents, especially how the church their parents were to be married in had flooded on their wedding day, and because of the flood, the vicar had had a heart attack and died.

'When I was young, a woman I loved broke my heart. We'd been childhood sweethearts. I wanted to marry her and live with her always, but I was poor. She was beautiful, and I wanted to give her the best of everything, so I took a job in the mines at Mount Isa. Two years in the infernal Australian heat, and when my time was almost up, I got a letter, telling me that she'd married someone else. I won't deny it was a dark time, the worst of my life. In my anguish, I decided to try and become a priest. So I went to France to spend some time in a monastery. You work hard in a monastery. You get up at two in the morning for the first of seven daily services. Ever been up at two in the morning, girls? No?'

Nicki rolled her eyes.

'In between services we did manual work all day, often outside. I'd never been anywhere so cold. I'd never seen snow, but in France it lay thick on the ground. Thick on the ground. When I had finished my six-month stay, the monastery sent me off to make my way to the train that would take me to Paris. I was carrying my bag and walking along in the snow and I felt so tired, so low. I had never in my whole life been so wretched, and then a car pulled up, a top-of-the-range Mercedes, and inside it was a gorgeous woman. She could see I was tired so she offered me a ride.'

Sarah saw the corner of Nicki's lip rise a fraction.

'When we got to the station, all the trains had been cancelled,' Jem spoke softly, 'because of the snow, so the woman asked me if I would like to go with her to her apartment. As I said, she was older than me but still a very beautiful woman. Believe it or not, I used to be quite good-looking...'

He's ugly, Sarah thought, with that black hair and those weird blue eyes like a jackdaw's eyes in a drawing she'd seen, and she knew by the way Nicki shifted minutely next to her that she thought so too.

'So I told her I'd be very grateful if I could rest somewhere for a while,' Jem went on. 'Her apartment was full of beautiful furniture, beautiful things. She lit the fire, opened a bottle of red wine and lay down on a rug. "Come and lie down with me here. Lay your head between my breasts and sleep for a thousand years."'

He looked at them and nodded. 'That's exactly what she said to me, "Lay your head between my breasts and sleep for a thousand years."'

Next to her, Sarah thought she heard Nicki mutter, 'Gross.'

Raising his glass to his lips, Jem sipped. 'So. Is that original enough for you, you spoilt little bitch?'

Sarah saw Nicki stiffen, her fists clenching as if she were about to leap up and attack him.

Veronica was making her way back to the table, swaying a little, holding on to the backs of chairs. 'What have I missed? What have you been telling the girls, Jem?'

The shopping mall, under strip after strip of fluorescent light, was too bright.

'I'm pissed,' said Nicki. 'Are you pissed?'

'Completely. My knees keep wobbling. Look.' They had loosened, become puppet-jointed, as if Sarah were practising a comedy routine. 'I am never drinking a martini again.'

They looked around the department store at the racks and racks of clothes, floors of clothes above and below them, room after room stretching all around.

'I wish we could go home,' Nicki said.

'I'm going to be sick.'

'Not here. Not on the carpet. Come on, Sarah, not on the carpet. Oh, no. Oh, Jesus. Are you finished now? God, Sarah, I've never seen anyone barf so much. Can you stop shaking? Come on, Sarah, stop it. Sit down for a minute.'

'I don't feel very well.'

'No kidding. Oh, Christ alive. What should we do?'

'I don't know.'

'Put your head between your knees. All right. How's that? Feel any better?'

'Not really.'

'You better have some coffee. Iced coffee, maybe. How much money have you got?'

'Veronica gave me twenty dollars. It's in my purse.'

'We have to wash that purse. Actually, let's just get the money out of it and bin it. She gave me twenty dollars, too. We can get lots of stuff with forty dollars. Can you remember what time Veronica said to go back to the restaurant?'

'She said, "Don't come back for at least two hours." She said if she wasn't there to get a taxi back to her house.'

'Oh, God, Sarah. Are you ever going to stop? That is gross.'

13

The child is silent as they cross the pass and descend into the valley. Sarah wonders what he is thinking, what his memories of this journey will be. On the outskirts of the town, she turns her head away as they drive past the white dust road where the house that her father built – the house that until recently was partly hers – still stands.

She has been so lost in her thoughts that she has not realised it is late afternoon. Whether she likes it or not, it is probably best that they stop here for the night. But in Orua, it is the weekend of the annual agricultural show. The place is heaving, almost as busy as it is on New Year's Eve. The campground is stuffed full of tents and trailers. A Ferris wheel rises from the domain. Tractor metal glints.

Outside every motel they pass, red neon 'No Vacancy' signs shine. At the fifth motel they try, a woman takes pity on them. She tells Sarah to come back later; there is a room but the occupiers have a late checkout. They're welcome to it but can't check in till eight that evening.

The child seems quite happy, subdued even, until Sarah says, 'Maybe we better get back in the car. Drive on somewhere else.'

'I don't want to go back in the car. It's too hot. We've been in it all afternoon. I want to go in the swimming pool. At the motel.'

'We can't, I'm afraid. We can't go back there until later.'

'The pool had a slide. It was really cool.'

'Don't get upset. Please. Come on, now. Why don't we swim in the lake?' In a burst of inspiration, she adds, 'We could go to the river.'

The truth is that she does not want to be here. And it makes it somehow worse that the whole town is celebrating, as uncaring a backdrop to her misery as it ever was.

'This is more like it.' The child is gazing at the silver curve of the water sliding through a guard of willow trees. 'Can I go in?'

'For a paddle, maybe. The current's very strong. See how it swirls around the boulders?'

Looking at it now, Sarah cannot believe that she swam here with her father when she was the child's age. Water flows between high black walls of rock before opening into a series of pools. To one side is a half-moon of silver river sand, on which Sarah and the child lay out their towels.

The child splashes ankle deep and then retreats,

yelping. 'The water's too cold. Can I go on the rope swing instead?'

'Let me test it first. It seems okay. It should be fine if you're careful. But don't swing too high.'

'Excellent.'

After swinging back and forth for a while, the child starts to build a bower of willow branches, planting the supple twigs in the soft sand, bending them until they meet, and then binding them together with wild grass stems. Around them, the air is full of the sweet scent of dog roses; already their hips are swelling and ripening, spheres of vibrant red among the dry grass, the purple-blue stands of viper's bugloss.

Sarah wades into the river until the water rushes over her thighs. She has forgotten how powerful it is, how strong and persistent its push. Though the child is playing happily, she does not want to be too far from him. The river water is so cold that before she expects it her lower legs are numb. Beyond the narrow gap in the rock, she can see the sun falling on the surface of the pool.

14

It was evening, and soon Sarah and her new friend Kitty would walk down into town to join the Orua street party celebrations in honour of the turn of another year. Except that this New Year was special. School was over, forever. In two months, they'd start university and their lives as adults.

Kitty sat on the sofa, peeling an orange. For the whole of that week, Kitty had eaten only oranges. The week before it had been corn, the week before that baked potatoes, although on the day they cycled on a disused railway line to Makata, in a brutal headwind, Kitty had also eaten two ice creams, one after the other. Kitty's skin was deeply tanned because her parents were currently staying somewhere in Western Australia, and Kitty had not long got back from sunbathing in the desert.

Kitty stuffed orange segments into her mouth.

'I'm going to put some pasta on.' Sarah put down her book.

'What time shall we go out?

'Not too early. Let's wait until dark.' The day had been hot; the earth, though cooling now, still released a punch of heat, heady with lavender. 'Do you want anything else to eat?'

'No. It'll bloat me.' Choosing another fruit from the bowl at her feet, Kitty eased her thumbs beneath its skin.

While the kettle boiled, Sarah stood in the kitchen, looking out on the white dust road and the houses opposite. Late sun poured in, heating the work surface. The boys who lived across the road were out on their driveway, washing and polishing their Falcons, soaping and then hosing clean the bonnets, working with their shirts off. There was a hatch in the wall behind her, opening into the austere, open-plan room where Kitty sat on the sofa, orange peel gathering on the cedar boards at her feet. Heat and oranges and lavender. The taste of Orua filled Sarah's mouth; it dazzled her brain with heat and light.

The pasta water was boiling, spilling out of the pan and over the hob, the element glowing red as Sarah lifted the pan off the heat. The scent of basil and pine nuts and parmesan cheese rose from the thick spoonful of pesto she stirred in after draining it. Cos lettuce, sliced cucumber and grated carrot waited, already prepared, in another bowl. Tucking a jar of olives under her arm, Sarah carried the food to the table.

'God, that smells good,' Kitty said. 'I'll just have salad. And the tiniest spoon of pasta. The *tiniest* spoon.'

Kitty ate the leftover pasta straight from the pot.

'Now I'll swell up like a balloon. Why did I do that? No willpower. Why didn't you stop me?' Kitty's chin trembled as if she might sob.

'You said you wanted some. Anyway, it's better to eat something before we start drinking.'

'What are you, my mother? It was the smell. I should have gone out when you were cooking and... oh, God. I've been in training for this night for the last three weeks, and I've just ruined it. Now I'll never get into my shorts.'

When Kitty ran off in the direction of the bathroom, Sarah got up and closed the door so she couldn't hear the heaving. Nicki had done the same so frequently her neck had swelled, and her eyes had been constantly shiny with tears.

Over the shush of the shower, Sarah heard a rush of tyres on gravel. She opened the door to see a car come to a stop with a soft hiss on the smooth concrete of the carport. A midnight blue MG, and behind the wheel... it looked like... Patrick! She'd barely seen him since he'd got that scholarship and moved away a few years ago.

'Very inconsiderate of you not to have a telephone,' he called through the open window, a wide grin on his face. 'I've driven all the way up from Port Glass.'

Long legs emerged from the car. White shirt. Jeans.

'How long has it been?' Sarah's smile was so rapid and wide it felt as though it might tear her mouth.

'Too long. Last Christmas, I think. This place just keeps getting better, doesn't it? You look well.'

He wrapped her in his arms, pressing his chin down on the top of her head.

'Who's this?'

'This. Oh. This is Kitty.' Kitty in a towel, picturesquely dripping in the low light, the whites of her eyes bright, the irises a dark, steel blue, her blonde, damp hair in a messy coil on the top of her head, the skin of her shoulders bronze.

'Hello, Kitty,' Patrick said.

When it was almost eleven, in the blue dark of midsummer, they walked down to the lakefront to join the crowds, Patrick trailing slightly behind Sarah and Kitty, his hands in his pockets, the same crooked smile on his face as on the first day Sarah had met him. Her heart was pounding painfully as it had when they had run together at school, despite the fact that they were merely walking, and downhill at that. Instead of the warm radiance of the white dust road, for a moment her feet felt as though they were sinking in dunes, cool sand pouring again into her shoes.

The crowd began to swallow them. Kitty was in front of Sarah, Patrick behind her. Sarah's house key, hanging on a chain around her neck, bounced and fell against her throat. There was too much pushing and pulling; they were being eased apart; the crowd, like a great stomach, was digesting them, breaking them to pieces.

Sarah called, 'Make your way to the jetty. I'll meet you there.'

Kitty swung off to the side, a bottle of Drambuie pressed to her lips. When Sarah turned to look, Patrick had vanished.

At times Sarah dropped to her knees and crawled between legs. The press of bodies pulsed above her and she became as clearheaded as if she had drunk nothing all night but water.

The jetty was empty, a place no one else wanted to be.

On either side of her the surface of the lake was a strange deep blue, covered with wobbling oval ripples, as if the water were made of shifting, liquid eyes. Sarah kicked off her sandals and sank to her knees, then lay with her back pressed to the still-warm planks, a throbbing like the music's beat, the crowd's din, rising through her from the soles of her feet and up, up into her chest. This was the moment, wasn't it? When the world would start turning her way; when the better Sarah nestled inside her would shine out, shine out and be seen.

The first chime of midnight. Sarah stood up. Where were they? She couldn't see them, only hordes of drunken strangers flinging arms around each other. Another chime. Where was Patrick? The striking went on and on and on. *Should auld acquaintance be forgot. We'll tak' a cup i' kindness yet.* And then, as if this were a play, in the tangle of bodies a window opened. Them. Him. Her. Pressed together, Patrick's hand in Kitty's hair, their mouths meeting.

Sarah jumped and the water closed over her head, cutting out sound. As her legs touched weed she remembered the eels she had seen one day from the jetty, their arm-thick shapes wavering around the posts. At the surface she gasped and began to stroke along the shore. When she was clear of the crowds, she climbed out of the lake and began to walk home, wincing as sharp stones and pine cones dug into the tender soles of her feet. It was a clear night, perfect for seeing shooting stars, but when she looked up at them all the stars were blurred.

Long ago, in the grounds of their school behind the sand dunes, with Patrick's penknife, she had carved her name into the smooth silver-white skin of a eucalyptus tree: 'Sarah' at right angles to 'Patrick', fusing them together, one shared 'r'. Ah, Patrick. It hurts. It hurts. It hurts.

15

Slumped in the back seat, the child says, 'I'm hungry'.

'Then we better find somewhere to eat. This look okay to you?'

Despite being phenomenally busy, the café happily caters to the child's whims, providing a bowl of pasta topped with cheese and broccoli for him. A side plate of raw, chopped vegetables. A salad to share. Some garlic bread.

She watches the child, wondering if his anger is going to flare, but he seems happy enough. When Sarah was a child, her parents had told her off for playing with her food. She remembers building a mashed potato volcano, studded with peas, a gravy-filled caldera at its summit.

Play was a doorway into better worlds where imagination was queen. Sometimes, when the child was small, to encourage him to eat them, she made the vegetables on his plate come to life, an army of little Frankensteins. The child's favourite had been Carrot Stick Man, who blew raspberries and was chased around the rim of the plate until captured and eaten. Slices of cucumber had metamorphosed into lily-pads, a spoonful of peas into frog food. Now she no longer needs to participate; he plays the games himself, acting out a little drama that ends in a crunch.

Pine nuts, basil, Pecorino cheese, durum wheat pasta, olive oil. The dry earth of a white dust road. Thyme and lavender and Kitty peeling oranges.

'What's the matter, Mummy?' The child, carrot stick halfway to his mouth, is watching her.

'Nothing.'

'You look sad.'

The child eats quickly then squeezes past chairs to the toy box. He comes back with a pottle of crayons and Sarah rips a blank page from her notebook, the one with the golden crown on the cover, and passes it to him. She flicks through the pages. Not much is written in it.

Ring.

The jetty.

Fantail.

Sometimes she has simply repeated the same word over and over.

Patrick. Patrick. Patrick.

The rest is all muddled: conversations with Patrick, dreams, memories, snippets of this and that. When she reads back over the entries, even though they are recent, they seem to have been written by someone she does not always recognise. Sarah picks at her food, looking out at what is left of the light.

When the child gives a wide yawn, she pretends not to notice. The café is filling up again with evening diners, the noise level growing uncomfortable.

'Shall we go?'

'Do we have to? I want to finish my drawing.'

'We can take it with us.'

'I want to finish it.'

Suddenly, she is desperate to leave. She feels as though people are staring at them, as though they might know what happened to her. Impossible. A few smile at the child, who is intent on his colouring, the end of his tongue sticking out slightly from the corner of his mouth. She feels sick with a kind of breathlessness, as if other people's happiness were a vapour that could choke her.

'Did you notice that ice cream shop we passed? Down by the lakefront. I wonder if it's still open.'

'May I have an ice cream?'

'Maybe. If you're good.'

They both know she will buy him an ice cream.

A curving pathway has been built along the shore of the lake, part boardwalk, part paving stone. A yellow seaplane rocks on the water. Dusk. The lake stretches away for miles. No lights in front of them, only behind. Laughter from pubs, bars, restaurants; the smell of frying meat, of spilt beer. At the ice cream shack, to Sarah's surprise, the child opts for vanilla. No flake. No sprinkles. They settle on a wooden bench and, as they look out towards the opposite shore, Sarah sees a small green light flicker on and begin to burn a hole in the darkness.

'What a coincidence. That green light over there. Marking the end of a dock.'

'What did you say, Mum?' The child licks his ice cream systematically, twisting the cone in his hands.

'It's just like a scene in *The Great Gatsby*. At the beginning of the book, two people are standing on a lawn, at night, looking over a sound, when they see a green light just like that one over there.'

'How can you look over a sound?'

'It's a different sort of sound. Not a sound you can hear.'

'I don't get it.' The child bangs his heels against the bench.

'A sound is the name of a narrow body of water that connects two seas. Or a sea and a lake.'

'Oh. Why is that important?'

'It's not important,' Sarah says. 'It's not important at all.'

16

Two months had passed since Sarah had kicked Patrick and Kitty out of the house in Orua on New Year's Day.

Sarah was back in Port Glass, crossing the quadrangle in the failing light of dusk, when she noticed his unmistakeable long, lean shape, pale-coloured in the near dark. Two paths crossed the square of grass from corner to corner in the shape of an X, and there he was, Patrick Creek, right in the centre where the diagonals met.

Images of the ugly scene that had taken place between the three of them flashed through her mind. Kitty crying and protesting that she'd been drunk, hadn't realised how much Sarah cared for Patrick. Patrick saying, 'What does it matter? It's not like we're an item, is it?' in that languid, careless way of his she recognised but with an edge of cruelty that was new to her. Inside, it felt as though a small but sturdy web, invisible strands of shared past woven from interactions and connections, had been swept aside, damaged, crushed.

Sarah was on her way to the Fresher's Ball. The theme was Bright Young Things, a choice that was bound to become rapidly more ironic as the night wore on. She stopped and started to back up, ready to turn and retreat. Too late. He must have heard the clacking of her heels, because he raised his hand and called, 'Sarah. Hey.' There was no choice but to advance.

'What have you come as?' Patrick, who had done his homework, wore a white flannel suit, a gold-coloured shirt, a silver tie.

Sarah found her dress in an op shop. It was the right era, black with a dropped waist, and a matching choker from which beads dangled, cold as they brushed against the skin of her neck, as if the night air had been trapped between them.

A widow, she wanted to say. Instead, she fumbled in her embroidered evening bag for her cigarettes, lit up and drew in a mouthful of smoke.

'You don't smoke.' As Patrick pushed his hands deep into his pockets, the corners of his mouth tilted downwards.

'Do now. Where's Kitty?'

'Over there. Throwing up in those bushes. She's been on the Marque Vue since five.'

'You?'

'Nah. Bit stoned, though. Have to be, don't you?' He took his hands out of his pockets, lazily gesturing at the lights of the hall glowing across the grass. 'Sarah, there's something I need to tell you.'

'I've got to go.'

'Sarah.' His hand was on her arm, holding her in place, next to him.

Patrick was going to tell her it had all been a mistake. He was going to tell her that all along it was not Kitty he had wanted to be with but her. Sarah.

'She doesn't know who Gatsby is.'

The cigarette idled between her fingers. She let it drop to the ground and crushed it beneath the pointy tip of her velvet-covered shoe. 'Who are we talking about?'

'Kitty. She said, "Was he that Russian novelist?"... Gatsby and Tolstoy muddled up?' He shook his head. 'She's fantastic, isn't she? Kitty, I mean.'

Oh, God. Was he serious?

'I know you were a bit angry about it at first,' he went on.

He waited for a reply, though none came. The nicotine swirled in her, and then she felt dizzy, as if she were suddenly on the point of being sick as well.

'But don't be. She won't stop being your friend just because we're an item, and neither will I.'

17

'Mum?' The child is pulling her arm. There is a ring of ice cream around his mouth, dribbles all over his hands, luminous white in the dusk.

'Oh. What a mess.' With a rush of air, the years zoom past her, speed over the lake, vanish into the darkness in the time it takes a small, green eye to blink. Pulling a tissue from her bag, she mops at the child's face.

'Can we go now?'

'Yes. Yes, of course.' Sarah shivers. 'The wind's got up, hasn't it? Are you cold?'

The wind is not cold. It is the warm nor'wester, the wind from Australia, the wind that sends demons to sleep. It is the wind that can free a young girl, tied up with magical ropes of dog-skin, from a monster's love. It is the wind that picks up the long muslin curtains that hang over Aunt Veronica's windows so they spin and twist until they tangle tightly, tightly together, as if it were too painful for them to be parted, as if they were trying to bind themselves until they had become one, an inseparable whole.

'I want to go to sleep.' The child shakes his head to and fro, at the same time banging his heels faster and faster against the bench.

'We have to wait a little while longer. The lady at the motel said we had to come back at eight. That's another half an hour. The room won't be ready for us yet.' But there should be a place they could go. Sarah and the child should be in the house her father built on that wildflower-strewn plateau, a long, low house with sliding doors, high-beamed ceilings and sparse, beautiful rooms, a house that smells of dry air and thyme and on every surface the finest coating of rock flour, which leaves white traces where it brushes against skin. The child's Lego should be spread out on the floor, waiting for tonight's dreams to inspire tomorrow's new additions, the net of stars in place above them and somewhere nearby the anchor of the moon, and the two of them safe and at rest.

'I want to go *now*!' The child is yelling. White drips fall from the end of the ice cream cone he has crushed onto his smooth, brown leg.

'Well, you can't. We have to wait.'

'I'm sick of this. I want to sleep in *my* room. I want to see Dad. I want to go HOME.'

The wind sucks at the last word, seeming to amplify it so that it spins around their heads before it's whisked away from them, lost among the steady thrum of waves on gravel, the sighing of branches, the distant thump of dance music from the lake-front bars.

'We *can't* go home. It's too far. Remember how long we spent at the airport? And flying on the plane? Think of how far we've come.'

'I hate you. I want Dad.'

His howls attract glances from passers-by, the half-sympathetic, half-suspicious looks aroused by severely distraught children. The last thread snaps.

'Stop it. Stop it right now. We have no choice. Do you understand?' She gets hold of his arm, ready to lift him and carry him across to the car. His answer is to bite her. With a yowl she drops him, all her attention on the gnashing pain in her forearm. Tears run down her cheeks and she raises her hand, ready to strike, shouting, 'You little bastard…'

The child is not there. His favourite T-shirt, teal blue, holds the faintest glimmer of light as his thin shape races away from her.

'Come back!' she calls, the tears still falling, pain dulled by a white burst of adrenaline. 'Stop! Please, stop! Oh, God, please stop!'

Her feet slip on the gravel and she falls. The stones are cold beneath her hands. She cannot see him anymore. The child is gone.

She is running in the darkness, calling his name as the wind throws her hair across her face. He doesn't answer. She's lost him, too, the thing most precious to her. The thought hits her hard, robbing her of breath as efficiently as a punch in the stomach, doubling her up. The water's wild now, whipped by the north-westerly. The thin, fine branches of the weeping willows sway, sweeping the gravel with their tips. When she was a child, she would run into them to hide, parting their branches like hair.

'The willows,' she calls, though there's nobody to hear her. Crouched at the base of the third tree down, she finds him.

18

On the morning after the Fresher's Ball, Sarah woke early, her grievances reactivated by her encounter with Patrick the night before. Some time ago, after saving up for ages, Sarah bought a typewriter from a second-hand shop. Almost immediately, Kitty asked to borrow it as she asked to borrow – in the name of friendship or perhaps as some sort of test – all the things Sarah liked and valued most. That was typical of Kitty: all take and no give. She'd borrow Sarah's clothes and give them back dirty and with tears in them, borrow Sarah's books instead of buying her own, ask to copy homework time after time after time. And now she'd done it with Patrick, taken him despite knowing how much Sarah cared about him.

Sarah stomped down to her car and drove to Kitty and Patrick's flat, determined to get her typewriter back. Why should Kitty get to keep it? As far as Sarah was concerned, they weren't friends anymore.

She tried the front door but it was locked. Beside it was a window. The curtains were closed but the sash window was open a fraction. Sarah rammed her fingers into the gap, hauling it up. She climbed in and planted her foot on the bed directly below.

'What the fuck? Sarah? What are you doing?' A familiar voice. Patrick.

'Sorry.' No, not sorry, actually; she gave the foot a twist before she hopped onto the floor. 'I didn't realise this was your room. Or I wouldn't have...'

'Mind where you put that foot, will you? Why are you here? Where are my glasses?'

'You wear glasses?'

'Contacts usually, but I wear glasses as well.'

'I didn't know that.' As she stepped to the side, reaching for the door handle, she tripped over a book.

'There's a lot you don't know about me. We've barely seen each other for the last few years.'

The room was tiny, not much bigger than an elongated cupboard. As she squeezed past, Patrick's hand whipped out from beneath the covers and caught her wrist. 'Wait.'

Don't look at him, look at the book. 'This is my book. I lent it to Kitty.' It was the sort of book Sarah liked, a fat tome about poetic symbolism. Trying to shake her wrist free from Patrick's grasp, she read aloud, '*In mythology, the god Jupiter is associated with both the oak tree and the terebinth. A two-faced god, Jupiter acts as a hinge between the past and the future.*'

'What? Like a swing door?'

'Don't be facetious.' Wasn't it the Oak King who was sacrificed every year at midsummer, the lame or wounded one? '*Venus is not the apple but the quince*. Talking of Venus, where's Kitty?'

'Aerobics, probably. Trying to burn off the hangover. Here's something I'm sure you'd like to know. When she realised I needed to wear glasses for reading, Kitty got a pair with plain glass lenses and started wearing them, too. She thinks they make her look intellectual.'

Venus has started wearing glasses, though she doesn't need to. Sarah knocked the book's spine on Patrick's knuckles. 'You really should talk about your girlfriend with more respect than that.'

'Ow. That hurt. Come on, give me a break.' He took his glasses off again, folding them closed, his eyes on her, widening them in some sort of plea. 'Ah, come on, Sarah. Come back over here for a minute.'

'I came to get my typewriter. Tell Kitty I've taken my book back as well.'

'When you recover from this little hissy fit of yours, let me know.' He turned away from her, pulling the duvet tight around his bare, bony shoulders. 'I'm going back to sleep.'

19

'Are you *sure* you're all right?' The receptionist, a weary-looking lady whose loose black clothing contrasts sharply with her white blonde bob, steps out from behind the desk. Before handing Sarah the key, she pauses to look them up and down.

Sarah can't see herself in the mirror, but the child – clinging round her neck like one of those soft toy monkeys with Velcro palms – looks a wreck: red-faced, wild-haired, tear-trails tracking through his dust-covered cheeks. One sandal is missing, the other dangles loose from the sole of his foot. 'We're fine. But we're very, um, tired. It's been a long day.'

The child comes round, groaning a little as she tucks him into bed. Sarah has a theory, as baseless as most of her theories about parenthood are, that with children, as with dogs, it is best to hide her fear. In as bright a voice as she can manage, she says, 'Goodnight, darling. Sleep tight. Don't let the bed bugs bite.' And don't ever, ever run away from me again.

'You always say that. What are bed bugs?'

'I'm not entirely sure. Remind me to look it up. Okay. Close your eyes. It's been a big day.' As she begins to rise, her knee joints crack.

'Mum?'

'What is it?'

'Did you forget?'

'Forget what?'

'You've forgotten, haven't you?'

Shit. Oh no. His lip is trembling again; his eyes are awash. 'Remind me?'

'This morning you promised you'd tell me a story tonight.'

'Did I?'

'When we were walking in the forest you said you knew a story about a fantail.'

'That's right. Okay. The story about a fantail.' Sarah wants to lie down. She wants to scream and she wants to sob. In all the furore, she has forgotten to ring Patrick. She wants to hear his voice. To speak to him. To tell him... well, *everything*. She takes a deep, deep breath and then releases it. She knows from previous experience that there is only one way out of this. 'You know I told you about the boy called Māui who had lots of adventures? Well, one day he decided that he didn't want to die.'

'Does everyone have to die?' The child looks up at her, duvet to nose, eyes widening.

'Um, yes. Yes, they do. So Māui thought, "How do I go about cheating death?" Now death was a very big absolutely terrifying goddess called Hine-nui-te-pō. That means Hine-nui of the night.'

'What does Hine-nui mean?'

'Something like "great lady". Māui knew he couldn't get near Hine-nui-te-pō while she was awake because if she saw him she'd flatten him with her great big fist or maybe something worse like eat him, munch-crunch-munch, so he said to himself, "I know, I'll wait till she's asleep and then I'll climb back up the way I was born. If I can get into her womb, then I'll never have to die."'

'What's a womb?'

'It's the place the baby lives before it's born.'

'And how do babies come out again?'

After three years of school, the child no longer considered the belly button a believable baby portal. 'From between the mother's legs.'

'Can you show me?'

'Er, no.'

'But wouldn't Māui be too big to go back up there?'

'You've got to remember that Hine-nui-te-pō was as big as a giant.'

'Oh. Yeah. I forgot.'

'Whenever Māui went on one of his adventures, all the birds of the forest followed him. Māui's best friend was a fantail called Pīwakawaka. And Pīwak-awaka was a great friend, full of fun and extremely cheeky. But this time, Māui had to be very firm with him. "Whatever you do..." Māui shook his finger at Pīwakawaka "... you must not, absolutely under any circumstances whatsoever, make any noise when I am climbing back up there, or else Hine-nui-te-pō will wake up and eat us or worse." "What's worse than being eaten?" Pīwakawaka thought but did not say. Instead he said, "I promise, Māui, I'll be as silent as a stone."

'So up Māui and the birds of the forest crept to where Hine-nui-te-pō was sleeping, and Māui climbed between her giant legs; first he put his head in and then his shoulders in and then his body in and then his legs in and his little feet were kicking around and it looked so funny that Pīwakawaka couldn't help it, though he put his wing over his beak: he laughed and laughed and laughed and Hine-nui-te-pō woke up and crushed Māui between her legs and... Māui died. So that's why everyone has to die.'

'What happened to Pīwakawaka?'

'I'm not sure. I expect he felt terrible about what had happened. But his children are still with us, aren't they? Laughing in the forest. Come on, now. Close your eyes.'

When the child is asleep, Sarah leaves his bedroom door a little ajar and sits at the table. She has turned all the lights out except one, a dim bedside lamp to act as a nightlight. She is too exhausted to move. She checks her pockets and her bag but she cannot find her mobile phone. She tries ringing Patrick from the phone in the motel room, but there is no answer. After putting down the receiver, she stares at the phone for a very long time.

A crushing weight seems to have settled on her chest, pushing the air from her lungs, squeezing her throat tightly, tightly. She tries to breathe slowly in and out through her mouth to fight the panic that's pressing down on her, but the weight remains. She's trapped here for the night, trapped here with memories she has run from for so long, which she has lived for years on the other side of the world to escape.

20

It was a couple of weeks after Sarah had gone to Patrick's flat and reclaimed her typewriter and her book. She had just come out of her botany lecture when, turning the corner by the museum, she saw Patrick leaning against a wall. He seemed to be looking at the trees which filled the park as their leaves spun in the wind, the undersides flashing silver. She clutched her books to her chest and forged ahead. He dropped into step beside her, saying, 'Sarah…' covering that distance between them in two strides of his long legs.

'What?'

'I sense some hostility in your tone.'

'Listen, I'm in a hurry. Is it something important?'

'Sarah, stop. This isn't like you. It doesn't suit you.'

'What do you care, anyway?'

'Listen. Just stop walking for a moment, would you? You know I care about you. I always have done. I know you're upset about Kitty. I wanted to talk to you, to explain.'

'Why? What's the point?'

'We've always got on well, haven't we? Ever since…'

'Ever since I thrashed you at tennis?'

'Ever since you showed your sporting prowess, despite the natural disadvantage of your tiny stature.'

'You had to bring that up, didn't you?'

'Come on, Sarah. We've been friends for so long. I thought if we could talk things through…'

There was something about the way he looked at her. There always had been. The icy wall inside her shifted a little as if touched by spring sun. 'Okay. You're right. We need to talk. But not now. I'm late for my archaeology lecture, and then I've got to go and see my mother. Some legal stuff to do with the house in Orua, now I'm eighteen.'

'Oh, Sarah. Oh, shit. It was your birthday, wasn't it? I knew I'd forgotten something. Everything's been…' He gestured to the leaves blowing round them in the cool and hectic autumn wind. 'Thing is, I'm going away tomorrow for a couple of weeks. That's why I wanted to speak to you today. But I'll call you when I get back.'

21

In the motel room, Sarah, sitting motionless at the table, hears the steady sound of the child's breathing. In, out. In, out.

If the child were not here, asleep, she would scream and howl and cry. Because she cannot, she swallows it all down but her breathing is harsh, strange. The pain in her chest has lowered and now it feels as though a block of dense wood is lodged under her ribs. She needs to calm down – but how? It's so stuffy in the room, so airless. As she moves over to the window to draw back the frail curtain and let some air in, she notices a sign of some sort on the door of the low refrigerator held in place by fantail-shaped magnets.

The sign is a menu for the minibar. But when she opens the matt silver door, she finds, in the cool, humming interior, not only a selection of miniature bottles, but full-size ones as well: two bottles of Aurora Pinot Gris, made at one of the local vineyards which line the river valley. After the child was born, she and James used to drink and argue all the time;

since he left them, she has barely drunk anything at all. The bottle is cool; a slick of condensation wets her palm as she eases it out and closes the door.

She finds a wine knife in a drawer. The wine smells of wet foliage, a hint of bush; thrown in among the alpine minerals, the sweetness of violets.

Sarah shivers; she can feel the darkness pass over her, wrap itself around her. The child is safe, is found. So why does she still feel terrified? A draft of cool night air from some unseen crack or the open window, from beneath the wooden weight of the closed, locked door rises up her calves and she is seven again, standing knee-deep in the river, watching her father swim towards the gap in the rock. The long-ago sun is hard on her shoulders, hard on her head. She sees her father surge through the water, arms whirling, beating like the wheel of a paddle steamer, but time and again the current pushes him back. The smell of the river is old and mineral; the grey sand is silky between her toes. Up he powers, arms a blur – almost there, almost there, yes, yes, no – his grip on the sheer rock slips.

The wine, cool and fragrant, soothes the tightness in her throat and chest. It loosens and shifts the wooden block in her chest until, balloon-light, she begins to float. It is as though she has stepped to the side of herself somehow, that her pain-wracked body and mind are hers no longer. Even sound is muffled. Another glass to dull the pain, drown out the fear. Almost there.

When the bottle is empty, Sarah finds herself standing up. She closes the window, draws the curtain, leaves the light on low. On a page torn from her notebook, she scribbles a message. Outside, she double-locks the door and slips the key into her pocket. Numb to her core, she is walking in the darkness, the nor'wester howling round her, working itself into a storm.

Through breaks in the cloud, two ultra-bright planets are visible over Quick Peak, at the head of the lake, lined up almost with its summit. Yesterday, when she had turned on the television to watch the weather report, the forecaster had said that the planets may be visible in the night sky. Jupiter: solid and soluble, oak and terebinth, ruler of sea-beasts and birds. And Venus: the rose, the quince, the cherry blossom, goddess of the terrible thing called love.

Sarah passes a great glass-box house lit up like an aquarium, where a man and woman sit at a white table beneath a chandelier, and somehow the darkness is the true light and the lights inside the glass house seem as out of place on the dry, white earth as water. Near the end of the road is a new estate of houses, enclosed by high iron gates.

And then Sarah crosses the road and is where she stood at seven, chest-high in the wildflowers. The tattoo-blue ghost house in the architect's drawing had risen from its skin-thin paper and emerged, long and low, built of sandstone the colour of pale honey, a tone or two lighter than the tussock-covered hills, a tone or two darker than the white dust, breath of glaciers, that coats everything here: leaves, road, skin, and now the lining of her aching throat.

And then Sarah is walking past it, looking in from the darkness to another lit window, the wind moving restlessly, warm all around her, the wind that sends demons, and in the place where she's so often stood is a man with a bald head, perhaps preparing something to eat on the kitchen counter, the counter she used to slide across in the morning so that her back was in the sun. Children's drawings cram the fridge door; the same cooker still is fixed into the wall; the room behind, visible through the hatch, always so austerely beautiful, is cluttered. On the driveway is a huge pile of firewood, and a large trampoline with a net around it. Then the man with the bald head stops what he is doing and looks up at her and her heart feels as though it's been torn from her chest and now lies there in front of her in the white dust. And yet she does not die. How does she not die? She walks past and then, at the end of the road, she turns and retraces her steps past the house, head lowered this time, not looking in but taking what she can, in terms of memory, away with her.

Crossing the reservation onto the flat plain at the foot of the lake, she sees that, in that short space of time, Venus has set. Jupiter is still there. Over Quick Peak, a little to the right of the summit, hangs a star cluster, and she wonders if she is seeing a galaxy or nebula, whether it is even possible to see something so distant with her stupid, flawed, human eye.

As she reaches the motel car park there's an odd lull and then the wind changes direction. The air's cooler now, cold almost, driving up from the south. As she opens the door, a burst of rain clatters on the cars. Inside again, her heart begins to thump, her numbness to thaw. When she sees the child, she starts to cry. How could she have left him? It was as though she could not help herself. She had not wanted to come to Orua but, once here, she had had to see. There is a kind of pressure building inside her. She is holding her breath, as if she were under water, and it is suddenly vital that she does not open her mouth, because if she does she will gulp the river, the lake, all of the vast blackness into her lungs and then it will always be there, inside her.

Sarah tiptoes into the child's room; she wants to reach out and touch his bronze hair, to find comfort by feeling the still velvet softness of his skin. Her hand reaches towards him and stops: has she learnt nothing?

There is an empty glass on the table. She has not yet travelled the necessary distance, needs to get further away from herself still. Sarah opens the other bottle and pours and sips: violets, chalky minerals, something with a taste so smooth that it is almost oily. In the darkness, she sits at the round table and drinks in steady drafts.

The room is all shadows. A car passes by, the sound of its engine amplified by the surrounding hills. The wind is thrashing rain against the windows, making the tree boughs groan. Her glass is empty again; she fills it.

When she tries to think about how she feels, the only thought that comes is that she has jumped into the dark lake water and she is swimming again, as she did that long-ago New Year's Eve. But instead of staying close in, this time she has turned her back on the crowds and gone out, far out into the lake. She is cutting through the water; it is slipping smoothly over her body. She is heading for the other shore, to a beach no one has ever walked on before, where the forest comes right down to the water, down so far that the beech branches hang into the lake and the steep sides of the mountains rise steadily to the peaks. She goes back to the fridge and fills her glass again, and then once more.

22

Sarah's gaze remained fixed on the picture behind the lawyer's chair. It was a painting of a range of hills, an angel and a rainbow. The angel and rainbow filled the sky space; the curve of the rainbow seemed to be pressing the angel downwards until its white-robed body almost touched the land.

'So now you and your mother and sister will each own a third of the property. Is that clear, Sarah?' the lawyer said. 'And this mortgage agreement. It's for three thousand dollars, but your mother will pay it back and then the property will be debt free again.'

'Maria deserves a new car. A mortgage is much cheaper than one of those car loans,' Nicki said.

Maria, her mother, and Nicki, her sister, leaned forwards in their chairs.

Her mother signed and then her sister Nicki signed and then they passed the paper to Sarah. Her mother did not look at Sarah but smiled and hummed, smiled so hard her eyes disappeared to crescents.

As Sarah pressed the pen onto the paper, the humming noise grew, filling her head, growing louder and louder. As if the movement might dislodge the sound, Sarah shook her head once, twice, three times, lifting her eyes to the angel, the waiting land, the weight of rainbow. The angel's expression was neither happy nor sad; if anything, it was indifferent.

23

When Sarah wakes she is on top of the covers, fully clothed, the side of her head sore and cold from being pressed against the wall. The child is on the floor, books and pencils and bits of Lego sprayed out around him. He rolls little metal cars up the slope of an angled book so that they fly over the edge before crashing onto the carpet. Though muffled, the sound is almost unbearable. Sarah tiptoes around him, hand on the white-painted breeze block wall to hold herself steady. In her mouth is a wretched dryness; when she pulls milk from the fridge, the centimetre of wine left in it slops accusingly. An empty Pinot Gris bottle stands by the door.

The tea tastes sour no matter how much sugar she adds to it. She does not even like sugar in her tea. The sound of the child crunching cornflakes makes saliva pool ominously in her mouth. Standing under the shower, she presses her head against the tiles and prays to a God she doesn't believe in to help her.

Mid-morning, as Sarah and the child check out of

the motel, her hands are still shaking. Her head feels heavy, as if it were made of marble. It throbs so much that, as they step out into the vast, unflinching light, it causes her to wobble. It takes her a moment or two to realise that the shrieking, crashing noises she can hear are not an interior soundtrack, the background music to her internal litany of self-scolding for the utter stupidity of drinking far, far too much.

Instead, somewhere nearby, drills sound; jack-hammers tear through some substance until it screams as if tortured to the point of endurance and then, quite suddenly, stops. For a moment or two, peace sweeps over her. The wind has dropped. Last night's storm has passed, leaving in its wake a pristine alpine day.

As they climb into the car, the child says, 'Where are we going today?'

'Port Glass. To see Patrick.'

'How long will it take?'

'A few hours. Five maybe. We have to take a longer route than usual because of the diversion yesterday.' As they walk to the car, a view of the lake and mountains opens up in all its heart-breaking beauty.

'Hey, look. Wow!' The child tugs her hand.

'What?' She follows his pointed finger and sees a small plane practising death spirals over the lake.

'That is so cool.'

He makes no protest about going in the car; in fact, he seems subdued, as if he were still exhausted by the events of yesterday.

This morning it is as if the old spirit – the one that has been with her since she was a child: the one that has kept her going for all these years through so many upheavals – has finally been kicked out of her. She feels as one of the child's creations might feel when, dissatisfied with the outcome, he ruthlessly disassembles all the bricks he had so carefully pressed together, tearing them apart and hurling them on the ground.

'Is there a playground in this place?'

'Actually, there's an excellent playground,' Sarah says, slowing the car. 'Down by the lakeshore. Want to see it?'

'Look at that!' The child gazes for a moment at the swings and a fancy wigwam-shaped climbing frame made out of rope. A series of brightly painted animals wait on thickly coiled steel springs for children to climb on and ride – a kiwi, a dolphin, a tuatara. And then he sees an enormous concrete elephant slide, and he begins to run towards it.

It's the same slide she played on as a child, though it's no longer painted lolly pink but gunmetal grey. While the child races around, she wanders down to the lakefront to look for her phone. Last night's rain has caused the lake level to rise and now the stand of willows where she found the child has water lapping around the base of their trunks. Ah, well.

She has had that phone since the child was born. Goodbye, phone. Goodbye photos of the three of them when they were a family, and of the more recent photos of the child and Sarah only, heads pressed tightly together, smiling.

24

It was two weeks after the visit to the lawyer's office, eight in the evening, and Sarah was in the kitchen with Maria, washing the dinner dishes. Sarah should have left home and been living in a flat by now. She and Kitty had planned to share. But after what had happened on New Year's Eve, Sarah had broken her side of the agreement and lost her deposit. By the looks of things, Patrick had taken her place. In between lectures and part-time work, she was searching for another room, without luck as yet.

The phone started ringing and Maria answered it. The caller's voice was so loud, Sarah immediately identified it as Veronica.

'Who? Jem? What do I care?'

Sarah heard Veronica's voice go up another gear.

'I'm not making a special trip up there to see him. I'm not spending any more time in any hospital. I don't care if he wants me to.'

Veronica was shouting so loudly that Maria held the receiver away from her ear.

'Tell him what you like. I'll never forgive him.' Maria slammed the phone down. 'If it rings again, don't answer it.'

'Was that Veronica? What's the matter?'

'Nothing.'

'I heard you mention Jem. Wasn't he that funny bloke who used to stay with Veronica? He told us a strange story once, about this woman who picked him up and seduced him in France. Wildly inappropriate tale to tell two young girls, now I come to think of it.'

Maria made small humming noises and then asked, 'What did he say?'

So Sarah repeated all she could remember of what she'd heard sitting in the restaurant lined with silver wallpaper. Jem's love for the beautiful woman who betrayed him; his life of misery in the mines; his trip to the French monastery and the walk through the snow; the woman opening her car door to him, and then later asking him to lie down and sleep between her breasts for a thousand years.

Maria's response was a silence, glacially cold.

'What's the matter? Have I said something to upset you?'

Maria said nothing, her face closed and still except for a quiver from tight-pressed lips.

'You seem upset. I didn't mean to say the wrong thing.'

'Shut up. You're vile. You're horrible. You're going to be a horrible person and have a horrible life.'

Maria's mouth barely moved when she spoke, as if her jaw had locked almost completely shut.

'But I don't understand what I've done.'

The chair Maria threw at Sarah hit her shoulder and upper arm and hip; its legs connected with her knuckles, the tender bones of her right hand. A little higher and it would have hit her head. It was the type of chair, brown, varnished, faintly Bavarian in style, that Sarah always thought of as fairy-tale furniture.

Outside it was cold and wet. Sarah ran out into the darkness, forgetting her coat. In the case of an emergency, leave your personal possessions behind. She ran until she saw the lights of the police station down by the docks. She had always wondered why the light illuminating its sign was such a sad, cold blue. Why was the colour of the light, of the mind, the colour of Kitty's eyeliner, also the colour of justice? Wind drove rain up the throat of the harbour, choking the neck of the causeway. Waves streamed over the road, the water thrown up into the air with a roar and then a silent pause before the thump, the shattered, shallow flood. She turned back, not wanting to have to walk through vast puddles on the footpath before her.

She rang the bell of the flat that Nicki lived in, and her sister came to the door.

'Why haven't you got a coat on, Sarah? You're soaking. Come inside.'

Nicki had that look on her face, her usual mixture of annoyance and antipathy. 'Are you busy?'

'It doesn't matter. Come in, Sarah.'

Would the police ask Sarah why her mother didn't love her? Would they ask her what she had done to deserve it? There had been some sort of crime committed, but who was the criminal? At school, counsellors from the Women's Refuge had visited her class. If someone hits you, it is always wrong. Even if they say they are sorry it will happen again. It will happen on average thirty-six times until the person being hurt has had enough. If it happens even once it is too often. You must leave. Even if they tell you that they love you. Even if they tell you that they're sorry. Sarah could not remember Maria ever telling her that she loved her. And Maria never said sorry.

25

After leaving Orua, Sarah and the child make frequent stops, finding the playground in every small town they pass through, Sarah drinking bottle after bottle of water and the occasional lemonade, swallowing the maximum dose of paracetamol and ibuprofen, trying to hold her hands steady on the wheel.

As they move eastwards towards the coast, the dry, golden countryside seems, at times, suspiciously empty of other cars. Where is everybody? And then the hills, lowering towards the sea, grow green. They need to stop and get something to eat for lunch, so, reaching the coastal motorway, they turn southwards only to find a row of police cars and a fire engine blocking their way. Sarah rolls down her window.

'What happened?'

A police officer approaches her. 'A landslip. It's all mudstone around here. Not the most stable stuff. All that rain last night must've washed the hillside loose.'

'We're heading to Port Glass. What should we do now?'

'Not a lot of options. You could get there eventually on the back roads but most of them are pretty rough. We're only advising that course of action if it's absolutely necessary and you don't mind your nice new car taking a battering. How urgent is it that you get there today?'

'Not very,' Sarah says. 'It's not really that urgent.' If she damages the hire car, she'll have to pay for it, too. Disappointment first and then a gush of something like relief. Not yet. A little longer. No need to face it, to face him, yet. 'How long do you think till it's cleared?'

'Could be one day, could be more. Best check in the morning.'

They turn and, once the traffic is moving again, head north. After ten kilometres or so, Sarah sees the sign for the next little settlement up the coast. As they turn off the motorway, a shiver of déjà vu passes over her.

'This is a nice place,' the child says as they drive in through a row of little houses tucked into pockets of bush. 'Are we staying here tonight?'

At the thought of last night's debacle, her head starts to ache and she moves her neck from side to side; her shoulders feel as hard as boards.

'Yes,' Sarah says, suddenly exhausted. The word sounds as hollow as she feels; burnt out, with the crumbling, smudgy lightness of charcoal. The little bay is the comforting shape of an enclosing arm, the water within it still and clear. After finding a motel, realising the child needs a run and she needs to stretch the cramp out of her shoulders, her legs, they decide to walk out of the shelter of the bay onto the headland.

Below the lighthouse, penguins are coming in from the sea. Slump-shouldered as if with weariness, they hop across the coarse, orange sand to the foot of the cliff. The Belgian tourists who precede Sarah and the child in the bird hide tell them that the penguins seem to come ashore at roughly fifteen-minute intervals. They settle on the wooden bench, looking down a slope covered in flax and broadleaf shrubs, and wait. Ten minutes pass, then twenty.

'Where are they?'

'Patience,' Sarah says, suddenly full of doubt.

'There!' the child shouts. 'I see it. Can you?'

'Yes. How wonderful.' As the penguin surfs in and lifts itself from the sea, Sarah's eyes fill with tears.

'Another one,' the child shouts. 'And another! Two more! Why are you crying?'

'Because I'm happy,' Sarah says. 'It's been a very long time since I saw penguins. Too long.'

'We've seen five already.' The child turns to her, flashing fingers. 'They only saw three. So we beat the Belgian people, didn't we?'

'It's not a competition. But yes, we did.' The penguins' feet are pink, curled, vulnerable as fingers. The blasts of sea air have helped to relieve the pain in her head, the dull coastal light has eased the strain on her eyes, but at the sight of the penguins, more and more emerging from the waves, the remnants of her hangover evaporate. Each waddling body fills Sarah with a bolt of head-lightning, a bubble burst of elation. Another safely home and then another. Triumphs of this kind are so rarely visible.

For a whole week, years ago, she and Patrick and hundreds of other school children planted thousands of flax bushes on a seaward headland near their school, dog-proofed with wire, the penguins' first sanctuary. Sarah can still feel that time inside her, the sea at their backs, the wind from Antarctica smelling of ice, and the deep, living ocean trying to flatten them as it flattened the fronds of bronze flax until they lay almost on the ground, shining as if the wind moving ceaselessly over them were a brush. Sarah worked next to Patrick, her nose, the back of her neck, her lower arms reddening with windburn, with sunburn, the freckles on her skin darkening, until they resembled the negative image of a star map. When Patrick was that age, he had smelt of dust and salt, and his skin had been lightly brown, his fingers fine and long.

'What funny feet the penguins have. Do you see?'

Harsh cries in the flax bushes, right beneath the hide.

'Down there, it's right down there.'

Looking up at them, a yellow eye.

The path leads down to the far end of headland, an old pā-site, desolate mudstone cliffs, weed-littered sand. Further south, beyond a rattle of boulders, is a beach. A group of horses run on it; they are chained together, practising for the races. Along this stretch of coast, not far from where she grew up, the sea air is different from anywhere else she has ever been. Sarah draws in a deep breath of it. *This is the wind I remember, the wind that knows nothing of land.*

Grass, dead and white at summer's end, stands as high as the child's shoulders. Narrow paths meander through it. Above the grass, a beak. *Hoiho hoiho.* Two penguins waddle onto the path in front of them; the same-sized child, arms clamped to his sides, waddles after them.

'Not too close; remember the sign.'

The child gives her a look. The penguins slide under the fence, ignorers of human boundaries.

'Twenty-two,' the child says. 'We *so* beat the Belgians.'

26

'What's going on, Sarah?' Nicki sat on the sofa, smoothing her skirt over her knees.

During most of their adolescence, the only things that seemed to give Nicki pleasure were her albums, full of unflattering photographs of her friends. Unlike most people, Nicki ripped the happy, smiling photos to pieces, and pasted in only the bad pictures – the grimaces and the gurns, the ones where eyes were red-pupiled or closed – adding beneath each snap a snarky caption made of odd-sized letters cut from newspapers and magazines, blackmailer-style. But Nicki was the one who had had to take responsibility for Sarah when Maria sent them away, every school holiday, to stay with Veronica. Nicki understood when Sarah, homesick, cried at night because Nicki didn't like staying there either. And more recently when (for no apparent reason but with increasing frequency) Maria was in a dark, fathomless rage, Nicki sometimes looked out for Sarah, in her own rough fashion. But this went beyond anything that either of them had seen.

'What is it that you want? And why are you so wet?'

'Maria threw a chair at me.'

'Why?'

'I don't know. Veronica rang while I was helping Maria wash up. Maria didn't say it was her but you know how loud Veronica's voice is. They were talking about that guy, you know, Jem, the creepy one who used to always be staying with Veronica when we visited? I ended up telling Maria about that weird story he told us that time. You remember, about the French woman?

'No,' Nicki said. 'I don't remember that.'

'And then Maria just... she just... went completely mental. I'm scared. I can't stay there after that. I was going to the station.'

'No trains this time of night.'

'The police station.'

'Don't do that,' Nicki said, a put-a-brave-face-on-it smile breaking through her frown. 'There's no need to do that. You better stay here for the night. I'll get you a drink.'

The next morning, Sarah pressed her fingers into the bruises, already showing faintly purple on her arm. Sarah pressed and pressed until it became unbearable and then she took her fingers off and the pain receded to a faint, pulsing throb.

At breakfast, Nicki was brisk, irritable even.

'What do you think I should do now?' Sarah said.

'How should I know?'

'I can't go back home. I can't live with Maria. And there are no rooms to let, not at the start of term. I've been looking everywhere...' Every time Sarah tried to think, her brain felt fuzzy, as though during the night it had grown a dense coat of fur, muffling her thoughts.

'Well, you can't stay here. Why don't you go away for a while? You're always talking about it. I'll deal with Maria. I'll deal with everything.'

'I've got some money saved up. There's a dig on. In Greece. They're looking for volunteers. My anthropology lecturer told us about it. I could go overseas for a while. Clear my head a bit. Let everything settle down.'

'That's a good idea. Hey, listen, Sarah, could you lend me some of that money? Just for a bit.'

'Are you sure you'll pay me back? Do you promise?' As she spoke, Sarah was seven again, her heart a stone sunk deep in her stomach.

'Of course I will. Why wouldn't I? Are you calling me some kind of liar?'

'No, that's not what I meant.'

'Let's go round to the cashpoint now then.'

27

Back in the village, they find a battered phone box half-hidden among flax bushes. Sarah sticks the phonecard she's bought into the slot, and, lifting the child, lets him punch Patrick's number out on the small, silver squares.

'Patrick?'

'Sarah? Where are you? Why didn't you ring last night?'

'Sorry. Everything's gone up the spout. I had no idea how much quake damage there would be this far south. We got stuck in Orua.'

'I tried your mobile.'

'Ah, sorry. I lost it last night.'

'How come?'

'Long story. I'll tell you all about it when I see you.' It's all still there, waiting: the lakeshore, the howling nor'wester, the child running from her into the darkness, her own walk past the house she lost, the wine. 'Then we tried to come south again this morning.'

'So where are you now?'

'On the coast. A storm moved over here last night. There was heavy rain and the motorway's been blocked by a landslip. We've ended up in a wee coastal place called Ariki. They say the road's not going to reopen for a day, maybe two. I'm sorry.'

'Typical, isn't it? We haven't seen each other for so long and now you're finally here there's this strange weather pattern. These problems with the roads.'

There's a hint of something in Patrick's voice; an old sound, not often heard, but familiar – she remembers it from school – the tapering off at the end of a word, as if his breath were running out, or he's turned his face to the side, away from the receiver. It's the way he used to sound when his team lost; the way he sounded after the one and only time she defeated him.

'How are *you* doing?'

'I'm... well, you know me. Impatient as ever. Looking forward to seeing you two.'

'We just saw the penguins coming ashore.'

'Twenty-two penguins,' the child shouts. 'More than the Belgians.'

'What was that? Did someone say something about Belgians?'

'Another long story. Listen, my credit's running low, but I wanted to let you know that we're on our way. That we'll be there soon.'

'I hope it's tomorrow,' Patrick speaks through the beeps. 'Sarah, do you remember that time when we...'

Before he has a chance to finish, the phone goes dead. Perhaps, like her, he remembers about planting the flax bushes for the penguins. Sharing memories like that makes her feel closer to him. Each time she speaks to Patrick on the phone, it seems a little unreal, as if she were still thousands of miles away when, in fact, the distance between them is now less than one hundred kilometres. She still cannot believe they are here, that she will see him soon. The fear that's gripped her, that sometimes loosens its hold but never fully lets her go, slips downwards for a moment, as if she were emerging back into the air after long immersion in a heavier element like water.

Patrick's voice lingers in her ear, and alongside it the sound of waves gently lapping against the piled-up stones of the quay, and then a watery exhalation as a massive seal raises its head from the clear green water and snuffs at them tetchily, following their movements with eyes that are wide, brown, and as bloodshot as a whisky-soaked gambler's.

On the end of the quay, Sarah notices a shack-like restaurant, cobbled together out of old timbers and corrugated iron.

'Shall we treat ourselves and eat in the restaurant tonight?' Sarah asks. The child has edged partly behind her, and, holding the back of her fleece, is peering out at the seal with a mixture of fascination and horror. Sometimes seals reek, but she can distinguish no particular odour from this one among the usual foreshore smells of decaying seaweed and iodine.

'Just you and me?'

'Why not?' She moves close enough to read the chalkboard menu through the window. A raw kind of hunger gnaws at her, perhaps intensified by the sea air, the tail end of her hangover.

'What sort of food is it?'

'Fish, mainly.' Sarah points at the dozen or so fishing boats, sleeping in the shelter of the bay. 'Those boats go out every day and then the people in the restaurant cook the catch.'

'Okay.'

The interior is dim, the walls painted a Rothko red-brown. The windows frame rectangles of sea and sky, glowing shades of slatey-blues, greens and greys under an overcast evening sky more beautiful than any painting.

Sarah orders blue cod for her and the child.

'Cheers.' When Sarah raises her glass of water, the child picks up his tumbler of orange juice. 'To the yellow-eyed penguins.'

'To twenty-two yellow-eyed penguins.'

'And to all yellow-eyed penguins we didn't see.'

The child looks at her blankly.

'Never mind. Just say cheers.'

'Cheers.' He places his glass carefully on the uneven wooden boards and starts reading.

I should tell him about planting the flax bushes, Sarah thinks. *If anything happens to me, there will be no one to tell him.* But Sarah says nothing, only looks out of the window at the receding shapes of the headlands in the distance, a signature design of this stretch of coast, a sight so familiar that the shape of them seems intimate, as if they were somehow part of her, or she of them.

On one wall of the restaurant is a mirror-lined cabinet. In it stand dozens of empty glasses, sparkling in the light cast down from row after row of little hidden bulbs. The child, following her gaze, says, 'Why are there so many?'

'They're for different types of drinks. See those big balloon-shaped ones? They're for brandy. And those tall, skinny ones are champagne flutes.'

'Flutes?'

'And those cone-shaped ones; they're for cocktails.'

'What are cocktails?'

'Special drinks, made with spirits.'

'Spirits? You mean ghosts?'

'No. That's what alcohol made from grain...'

But then the child holds up his hand, as if to say 'enough'. The food arrives and he starts cutting it up, the knife and fork over-sized in his small hands. Talking to the child makes words resonate again, shaking from them the dust of overuse. At times it makes her feel as if she, too, were a child again.

28

Last night at Nicki's, Sarah had rung the phone number she found on the scrunched-up flyer she'd ripped from the university notice board. A cheerful voice with an English accent, Professor someone or other, had answered. New Zealanders were hard workers, the voice said, and she would be most welcome to join their happy crew on the dig for a month or two.

In the morning, after waiting till Maria was safely at work, Sarah snuck home and packed a bag. The rest of the day was spent in a travel agency, arranging her route. Flight via Singapore, then Athens, then a ferry service from Piraeus, which would eventually drop her at a far-flung island in the Cyclades. There was only one possible connection a week, leaving tomorrow. Once she got there, all her accommodation and expenses would be paid and the cost of flights would be refunded, too.

It was late afternoon by the time she finished her necessary tasks and essential shopping. She didn't want to stay with Nicki again and risk the chance of being parted from any more of her money. There were a few little seaside places up the coast, though, not far out of town, each of them with a handful of houses, a shop and a motel. They were not far from the airport, which was on the outskirts, too. Heading out of town on the motorway, she saw the looming, bluestone bulk of Firdell Hall, and the bruises on her body began to thump. It had been months since she had last visited Nana.

'I want to see Mrs MacLeod,' Sarah said, after the nurse buzzed her into the reception area. 'I'm her granddaughter. I'm going away and I'm not sure when I'll be back.'

'Well, I'll need to check with her doctor first. Take a seat.'

Ten minutes or so later, the nurse came back and beckoned Sarah to follow her.

Nana was up at least and sitting in a chair. 'Ah, Sarah.'

'Hello, Nana.' No one's skin was as silky as Nana's, but it had turned the wrong colour, a shade of appalled white. 'They're worried it will upset you, me coming to see you.'

'Ah, Sarah.' Nana patted her hand.

'I love you, Nana.'

'Ah, Sarah,' her grandmother said.

Nana suffered from depression. She would not eat or take her medication because she wanted to die. Sarah's grandmother was in the private asylum to be force-fed.

'Listen to me, Nana. When I leave here I'm going to go and buy an axe. And then I'll come back and cut down all these bloody gloomy trees. If you look out the window in an hour or so you'll see me.'

Nana hated swearing. It always made her say 'och', or at least release a stream of high, curt, disapproving tuts. But not today. Nothing seemed to shake her out of this stupor, as if they kept her so heavily drugged that she could barely function.

'Ah, Sarah,' Nana said. 'Cut…' But then she stopped, mouth open, as if she had forgotten what it was she was going to say.

'When I've chopped down all these bloody pine trees, I'm going to make a big heap and set fire to them. It's going to be the biggest bloody bastard of a fire you've ever seen.'

'Ah, Sarah.' Raising her hand, Nana made a stroking motion in the air between Sarah's head and shoulder. 'Cut. She. Cut.'

'Oh, Nana. I'm sorry. I didn't mean to upset you. I'm not really going to cut down the trees. I just wish I could do something to make you better.'

'Ah,' Nana said, 'Sarah. Long. Long.'

'It's just that it's so bloody gloomy in here. You're never going to get better in this shithole of a place.' To emphasise the importance of this, Sarah reached over and, picking up Nana's fragile cluster of fingers, squeezed them as hard as she dared, before returning them to Nana's lap.

'Ah, Sarah. Long again. Your…' Nana moved her mouth, but the word eluded her. She looked down at her hands, folded in her lap, as if she had never seen them before.

'What is it, Nana?'

'Why?' Nana had tears in her eyes. 'Why?'

'Please get better, Nana. Because I love you. I'm going away tomorrow. You've got to get better. Promise me you'll get better soon.'

'Sarah.' Nana was suddenly agitated, trying to stand up. 'Sarah. Your hair.'

The nurse came in then and, with an accusatory glance, told Sarah to see herself out. At the first locked door, she should press the buzzer and wait for assistance. It was not difficult to sneak away on the padded carpet, but the sound of Nana's crying broke into her, working its way deep inside her as rain, falling on stone, works its way into a thousand cracks.

29

It is fresher on the coast than inland. The water in the swimming pool glitters coldly. Leaves float on its surface, little boats pushed to anchorage on the pool's sides by the child's splashing and Sarah's staccato breaststroke. In the kōwhai tree, a wax-eye flits until an obese wood pigeon, drunk on berries, crashes through a neighbouring pittosporum, frightening it away. Little breaths puff from Sarah's mouth: woh, woh, woh. *Don't get out yet, stay in the water; see how much you can stand.* The motel complex is the kind of place – slightly dilapidated, home built, basic – where they fill the pool in spring with the hosepipe and drain it again in autumn. Now it is light, she can see that there was once a painting of an octopus on the bottom of the pool but its colours have faded, some of its tentacles have disintegrated, the features of its once-smiling face have been scraped away in places so it seems to gape in horror, as the Medusa did at her reflection, in some agony of knowledge.

She has heard this morning that the road will not open today.

No matter how many laps Sarah swims, she cannot seem to get warm. She clambers out of the water and sits on the side of the pool, her feet and lower legs submerged, distorted, the sun warm on her back, mesmerised by the rippling pattern on the blue surface. The child is playing a different game today. His games are always changing. He climbs the three little steps and launches himself off, diving under water, swimming beneath it for as long as he can, and then surfacing, gasping, spluttering, flailing his arms. He is a good swimmer, but each time he does this, she wants to call out, *Careful, do be careful*. It is another phase, another level of danger, another tranche of testing. Like Patrick, who would hit ball after ball over the net, throw ball after ball into a hoop, kick ball after ball towards a goal mouth. The child does not understand how she can be content to sit there, merely watching.

'Come in and play with me,' he calls, but she shakes her head. After drying off, she walks over to a dirty plastic table, which wobbles unsteadily as she places her glass of water on it. Her notebook is open.

I only eat the olives.

Lay your head between my breasts.

It'll come back to you, you know.

Twenty-two penguins.

Tell Patrick I said goodbye.

As the sun climbs the sky, the morning's coolness disappears. They move into the shade of the veranda so the child can continue to play, sheltered from the rays of the late morning sun. The sea sounds gently below them in the bay. When the child wanders inside, rubbing his stomach, Sarah makes something to eat. After morning tea, Sarah asks, 'Shall we go for a walk?'

'Where to?'

'Further along the beach there are boulders. Big, round boulders. You can climb on them.'

'Really?'

'Look along my arm. Down there. You can just about see them. There, at the other end of the beach.' The tide is going out, exposing all of them that there are to see.

'I think I can see. Something blobby.'

The boulders vary in size from a few feet to three or four metres in diameter. They spill from the mudstone cliff to the tide line and on, out into the sea: concrete-grey, honeycombed with veins of yellow calcite, round as those other concretions, their smaller relatives, hidden in the soft, folding flesh of oysters, pearls. Around the boulders, the tide has left pools of light green water. The child climbs happily from boulder to boulder, clambering inside one that has broken open and pretending to burst forth, a chick hatching from an egg.

What a strange world, Sarah wants to say to the child, *isn't it?* But she says nothing. There is so much to tell him. But she doesn't want to overload him. She wants to tell him things that he will remember. Sometimes she wonders what use telling these stories has. Other times she thinks that they are all that matters. When everything else is gone they are all that we have left. Patrick was never a romantic, but even he once admitted to Sarah that the best stories are about love, whether they end happily or not. As she looks at the child, she tries to remember what she felt when he was born. And then she tries to imagine what it would be like not to love him, what it would be like not to love anybody.

It is not something she wants to think about. But she must try. It is almost as though she has come on this journey to imagine the unimaginable, to find the truth behind the smile of shame. Not loving is a fact, like boulders emerging from a mudstone cliff, like the fact of the sea. Like the star cluster she saw. She tries to keep her mind on it but her mind is shouting, *Wrong!* Her mind is running, a cartoon stick figure with hands over ears, screaming, *No, No, No!*

30

After leaving Nana, Sarah drove for half an hour or so, wiping at her eyes. Ever since the start of this year, it seemed as though whatever she said or did made everything worse. At the first small village, she found a motel with a vacancy sign outside it.

From her room, she rang the number Patrick had given her and this time Kitty answered.

'He's not here. He should be home soon, though.'

'Can you ask him to ring me, please? We were supposed to meet up today, but I couldn't make it. Something came up, something urgent.'

'He didn't mention that to me. Why were you meeting him?'

'There wasn't a specific reason. We decided to meet for a coffee, that's all. I guess the idea was to patch things up after... what happened.'

'We're happy, you know. You're not still trying to break us up, are you?'

'No, Kitty. Of course not.' Sarah told Kitty about her trip to the dig in Greece.

'Yes, I'll give him the message. Ah, huh. Okay. What was the name of the place you're staying? Okay.'

'If he can't make it up to the motel, I'll be at the airport at midday. My flight's at two in the afternoon. Please. I must see him.'

'Sure,' Kitty said. 'I'll let him know.'

After putting the phone down, Sarah stood looking out on the darkening sky. Beneath her window was an empty swimming pool, its corner slowly filling with autumn leaves. On its floor, the bright colours of a freshly painted octopus, grinning wildly, its tentacles waving.

So often it was windy on this coast, but tonight everything was still, so still. The disappearing sun left traces of light in the sky, streaks of rose pink, mint green, warm orange. Far out, artificial radiance from the Japanese squid fishing boats, false lights promising love, lured the pale creatures from the safety of the dark to the waiting nets.

Maria would be home by now and would have read her note.

The phone did not ring. Cars were few in this tiny place. Every time one passed, she thought, *Patrick*. But he did not come.

After Sarah checked in, she searched the airport, but he was not there either. She roamed about – it was so small a space – turning each time the electronic doors slid open, letting in gusts of sheep smell from the surrounding paddocks and occasional sweeter scents from the far, bush-covered hills.

Where was he? Why was he not here? There was only an hour, now half an hour to go before she had to board her flight. And then a familiar face at last, but not his, Kitty's. Perhaps he was outside still, parking the car. But then why would Kitty be twisting a bunch of keys like that, jangling them in her palm?

'Kitty! Thank goodness you've come. I was getting worried. I have to leave soon. And you told Patrick?'

'I did.'

'So where is he?'

'Not here, as you can see.'

'But why? If you told him what I said, he'll realise how important...'

'You're not the only person in the world who matters, you know.'

'I know that. But...'

'Will you stop talking and let me finish? Patrick didn't see the point in coming. We spoke about it last night. He said you'd go off in a huff and come back in a few weeks when you'd calmed down a bit. He said that was what you always did. You were too up yourself to apologise, though. It was everyone else who had to do that, bow and scrape before you'd even deign to speak to them again. You've frozen me out, haven't you? Just because Patrick preferred me to you...'

'You knew how I felt about him. I was always telling you about it. You didn't even think about my feelings…'

'What about *my* feelings. What about me? You think it's okay to look down your nose at me because I'm not as clever as you. Well, you're wrong. I'm a lot cleverer than you think.'

There was something in the way Kitty said it. Sarah tasted something bitter in her mouth. She clasped her hands together, to stop Kitty seeing that they were shaking. Sarah stood and picked up her bag.

'I've got to go now.'

'I won't stay and wave you off.'

'Goodbye, then. Tell Patrick I said goodbye.'

Kitty just smiled.

31

When they are almost back at the motel, the child touches her arm. 'What's that bird?'

It sits on the telephone wire, back towards them, head turned to the side. An azure and turquoise back, its breast cream with a wash of gold. Kōtare. *Halycon sancta vagans.*

'It's a kingfisher.'

'It's lovely.'

The kingfisher is undoubtedly watching them as much as they are watching it.

Unlike her ex-husband, James, for whom they were a minor (bordering on major) obsession, Sarah never dreamt of birds. But one night, years ago, when things were at their worst, Sarah had a dream that a kingfisher flew out from under the surface of still water and jabbed its beak into the side of her neck. So vivid was the dream, she can remember it in exact detail: how she grabbed hold of the bird's slightly slimy body, how its wings felt softly smooth, almost oily, against her palm, how the dull, radiant pain almost cut off her airflow, making it hard to breathe. It hurt like hell: the bird's beak was blunt, insistent, and surprisingly difficult to dislodge. She woke, sweating, arms flung wide, trying to fight off what she felt certain must have been an attempt to strangle her. But no one had been trying to strangle her. James had been gone for months. The child was in her bed but was curled in a ball, far away from her. And it was not even night but daytime, three o'clock on a winter's afternoon, the time Sarah and the child both usually woke from their afternoon nap.

After gulping down some water, her heart galloping, she lifted her fingers tentatively, exploring the space between her ear lobe and clavicle, discovering nothing more than a smooth, surprisingly soft expanse of skin. A further check in the mirror revealed a stretch of unpunctured epidermis, fish-belly white, speckled with a few stray freckles. Some days later, still haunted by the dream's strangeness, she looked up the symbolic meaning of kingfishers. And now here is one, right before her on the gently swaying telephone wire, a bringer of urgent messages from the unconscious.

On the way back to the motel, Sarah buys another phone card. Patrick has told her that he will be busy with appointments over the next few days so she is not surprised that he doesn't answer. She leaves a message, telling him they have been delayed for at least another day.

The child wants to play on the beach. Sarah spreads a towel out on the grainy, orange sand and

135

watches as he sifts through the offerings of a storm tide – great blue-black mussel shells, rose-shaped sponges, twisted ladders of violet-red seaweed, the bulbous club-like roots of giant kelp, sea-carved curves of fishbone, crab carapaces, sea-polished driftwood, rainbow-laddered pipi shells – each one picked up and examined and then placed separately, ordered into some sort of pattern, as if he were trying to make sense of the random gifts of the sea. Patrick. Ariki. The kingfisher, diving beneath the shifting mirror of the water, bringing its catch up into the light, into air it cannot breathe. Patrick's voice, sounding in her head. Patrick.

32

Greece was overwhelming: the light, and the close-by sea, the ceaseless wind, warm and dust-laden. The island was small and almost barren, with a few pot-holed roads and, scattered all around, what appeared to be piles of rubbish, both ancient and modern.

Sarah staggered off the small ferry to find that everyone from the dig was on a lunch break. A young local boy led her to a taverna by the beach, and she joined a group of sunburnt international students drinking beer and wine and sharing small dishes of cold, delicious food.

'Why are you so pale?' someone asked her, and she explained that no New Zealander in their right mind sunbathed, which seemed to puzzle them all but especially the Swedes. Lunch, she was alarmed to find, ran from midday to four in the afternoon.

They kept filling her glass with wine, and before she knew it, they were leaving for the next shift and she was hauling her backpack on and heading, none too steadily, in the direction of her hotel. The place was whitewashed inside and out, and all the rooms were accessed by simple wooden doors running off a long corridor. Inside hers, the wooden shutters were closed, letting in air but keeping out the sun's glare and creating a pleasant dimness. She tipped out her backpack and, grabbing everything she needed for a shower, scuttled down the corridor to the bathroom.

The water was cold, but it sobered her up a little. She wrapped herself in a towel and scampered back down to her room, suddenly exhausted. Odd that the door was slightly ajar; she mustn't have closed it properly. It was almost two whole days since she'd left New Zealand. She could rest properly now, after snatches of sleep on the long flight and ferry ride. Unable to see much in the dim interior, she dropped her things in a heap on the floor, lay down on the cool white sheets and slept.

When she woke up, a young man was staring down at her.

'Had a nice nap, did we?'

'Christ. Who are you? How did you get in here?'

'I might ask you the same thing.'

'It's my room. I just arrived today and… oh dear.'

The man opened the shutters. Evening light spilt on a desk, a typewriter and a pile of books which were definitely not hers, though the heap of dirty clothing on the floor, including summit-positioned bra and knickers, undoubtedly were. Even if she'd

tried, she couldn't have arranged them in a more em-
barrassing way.

Sarah jumped up and saw her wet hair had left
damp patches on his pillow. 'I'm really sorry. I was
tired and I must have got the wrong room. Um, I'm
Sarah.'

'They were right. You really are pale. We'll have to
see what we can do about that.' The man held out a
tanned hand. He wore faded denim shorts and a pale
green polo shirt with a crocodile sewn on the pocket.
'I'm James. Professor Robbins told me to expect you
today, but I must admit I didn't quite see this coming.'

'Oh, God.' As she scooped up her clothes and
hurried out, she heard a small metallic crash. James
caught up with her in the corridor.

'Your key. Allow me. Get yourself sorted out and
then come along to the taverna at eight. I hear you've
been there already.'

33

The road is open again. After breakfast, they pack their bags and get ready to leave Ariki. The sea, which, outside the shelter of the bay, has been so restless, is still, its colour pewter; faint citrus-yellow light seeps over the horizon.

It is about an hour's drive to Port Glass, but as each mile passes Sarah feels every part of her, especially the exposed areas – mouth, face, eyes, neck, scalp even – tighten, as if the diffuse light from the overcast sky were intense sun. The child is silent, staring dreamily out of the window at cabbage trees and salt-battered buildings with corroded iron roofs, dead and dying cars, trucks and tractors sinking earthwards in their grounds.

A pukeko darts from a swampy stand of flax, a slate-blue, red-legged streak, and races alongside the car for a moment or two before disappearing again between the blades of foliage. The hills around here are a strange yellowish colour and many are cone-shaped, as if they were a string of old volcanoes. The whole coastal strip looks defeated, bashed around by the relentless weather, and in places the road slumps unexpectedly. It's a relief when the road turns inland and passes through a small town. Though it's not far from the coast, the seaward hills' shelter creates a green valley with a clear fast river running through it. Sarah is tempted to pull over here, find a place to stop; any excuse to delay the last part of her journey.

She imagines he will startle at the sight of a swamp harrier lifting from a bloody pile of road kill as the car approaches, that he'll exclaim at the sight of its broad, tawny-brown wings, but that screen seems to have come down in front of his eyes again and, though he stares out of the window, it seems to her that he might as well be staring into darkness, so far away is his focus in thoughts, in imaginings. Ten years since she has been home and yet it all seems so familiar. The strange intensity of light; the deepness of the shadows. England's soft light, its gentle, muted tones of green and grey, its foxes and squirrels and badgers, feel impossibly distant, landscapes and creatures from storybooks.

The road touches the coast again beside the still waters of a gentle lagoon, a bar of pine-topped sand protecting it from the sea, and then the road rises for what she knows is the last time. The hills here are clad in dense forest and so high that, though the day is hot, faint mist hangs about bare outcrops on the summits. When she was young, she used to dream those broken rocks were the remains of long-ruined castles, ancient palaces.

And then they are beginning their descent of the long, steep hill into Port Glass. There is the pale grey harbour and, beyond the town, the green-white sweep of sea; waves break over Kapeka Island, throwing up plumes of spray.

She would like to drive straight out to the beach and see Patrick immediately, but the schedule has spun off course, all their plans gone awry. They should have been here already. Today Patrick won't be free to see them till early evening.

The motorway ends and they are in Port Glass, driving along the bottom of one of the town's many valleys. Sarah indicates, turning the car onto a winding road which passes the Botanic Garden. Further on, before the road ends at the shore of a little half-moon bay, Sarah pulls over and parks near a cluster of wooden houses.

The grass is damp underfoot; within the hedges of koromiko, the air carries a light tang of seaweed, salt. It's only a small cemetery; the hedges shelter it and trap the warmth.

'What actually is a cemetery?' the child says.

'It's a place where people's bodies are buried after they die,' Sarah says.

'Oh,' the child says. 'It looks like a garden.'

'Yes,' Sarah looks around, vision adjusted by child magic. 'I suppose it does.'

The low stone is covered in the unreadable language of lichen: it obscures the names and dates written beneath it, all that is left on this earth of her father. The lichen folds in on itself, fold after reflexive fold, as on the West Coast fiords probe fingers of sea into the land.

For a moment, Sarah looks at it. She looks at the dirty, empty vases standing nearby and realises that no one has visited this spot to clean and take care of it since she last did, more than ten years ago. And then she is on her knees, tearing at the lichen with her fingernails.

'Can you tell me the story of the cheeky fantail?'

'Not now. Mummy's tired. You know the story. Why don't you tell it to Sparkles?'

'I want *you* to tell it to me.'

'I told you, I'm tired.' Tearing away the lichen has caused Sarah to lose a layer of skin from the end of each finger. Everything she touches – the battered laminate of the pub table, the burning china of the child's mug of hot chocolate, the cold, curved surface of her glass – makes her draw in sharp breaths between clenched teeth.

'Your cheeks have gone red, Mummy.'

'Have they?' The wine, though cold, is cheap and sour. Chateau cardboard. Her resolution never to drink again has lasted two days. She gulps.

'Mummy?'

'Yes?' The child is a living seismograph, a fine silver wire trembling up and down her white page, recording every expression, every shiver of passing mood.

'Please?'

'I said NO.' Anger, blinding white, blasts through her. She will never tell him the story again; she will withhold what it is in her power to withhold. She is Maria, Destroyer of Worlds, Queen of Spite. The drunks in the bar turn and stare at her with knowing eyes.

Breathe.

Breathe.

Deeper.

Now slowly.

Slowly.

It is not his fault. None of this is his fault.

He is innocent.

Innocent.

Her foot slips and she kicks a wretched ficus plant. Barely more than a bald stick, it rises from an orange plant pot half-filled with dust-dry soil. 'I'm sorry, love. I'm so sorry. I love you so much. I didn't mean to shout at you. Please don't look at me like that.'

'Why are you crying?'

'Because I'm sorry. That I shouted at you. I shouldn't have shouted at you.'

'What are you doing with your drink?'

'I'm giving it to the plant. It looks thirsty.'

'Does it?'

'Right. Okay. Now. Where were we? A story. Once upon a time, there was a brave and adventurous boy whose best friend was a fantail.'

The vases, scrubbed clean in the pub kitchen for a small fee, stand beneath the headstone, full of flowers. Irises, freesias, forget-me-nots. The lichen is gone, thanks to a borrowed wire brush. Perhaps it was a foolish waste of energy to remove it, but now, if anybody aside from them should wish to do so, they can read the name, the dates.

'That looks better.' The child pushes some daisies he's picked from the grass into the water. 'If we can't take the fantail's nest home with us, perhaps we should leave it here.'

'What a good idea. This is the perfect place for it.' The same feeling, as when Sarah stood with the child and saw the penguins emerge from the sea, cloaks her.

The child rests the nest, grey-green as the stone, against the vases.

'"...birds build – but not I build."'

'What did you say, Mum?'

To root out and to pull down... to build, and to plant. Last night in the motel room, she'd picked up the Gideon Bible and, in an unthinking act of bibliomancy, opened it to the Book of Jeremiah. But the snatch of poem; where had that come from? 'I didn't say anything, did I?'

'I know what you were doing.' The child nestles close, slipping his hand into her pocket, mining for sweets. 'You were praying, weren't you?'

34

She'd been on the island for three weeks and James was laughing at her again. Good naturedly, admittedly, but that was all he ever seemed to do since the minute they'd met.

'But what do you mean, it'll take months to re-fund the cost of my plane ticket? How am I supposed to get home?'

'You will. Eventually. It's just that the wheels of the finance department grind slowly. And exceeding small, come to that. You need to send your ticket to the London office and wait for them to do all the paperwork. Relax and enjoy it whilst you're here. Your accommodation's paid for; you've an interesting job, sifting dust off old, broken things; you have excellent company.' James described his area of expertise as event aftermath and this is what they did all day, dig through what remained after some nameless, ancient disaster.

'I *am* enjoying it. I'm just worried about what happens in six weeks' time if I haven't got enough funds to get home.'

'Haven't you got anyone you could ask to send you the money?'

There was the money Nicki owed her, but the problem was how to get Nicki to give it back to her. 'It's almost impossible to make a telephone call. How on earth would I get someone to send money here?'

'Let's look into it. There must be a way.'

To telephone overseas, you had to get a ferry to the neighbouring island and go to the post office and stand in a long queue. Letters took weeks to arrive. The kind of happy chaos, which seemed to rule life, extended into public services and businesses alike. Hours were erratic. Nothing was computerised.

After taking a morning off work and queuing up for most of it, Sarah spoke briefly to Nicki, who said she'd send the money she owed. She visited the bank and asked for weeks, but no funds ever arrived in her account.

Sarah wrote to her mother asking for some sort of explanation or apology, but Maria's reply contained only vitriol, blaming Sarah for running off and leaving her without help, and pouring down more scorn, listing faults which, though largely imaginary, still tore wounds into Sarah.

She wrote to Patrick and phoned him. Whoever answered the phone said that Patrick and Kitty had moved out of the flat some weeks ago, and to her letters she received no reply.

35

Back on the main road, Sarah drives past the tall towers of the university and down the long street which bisects the town and leads seawards. The oldest parts of the original settlement, located far enough from the beach to miss the worst excesses of coastal weather, are hidden, almost, in a dip. Shops line the road, along with the occasional office building. Though most of the structures are less than four storeys high, this area has a shady, gloomy feel, as if they have stumbled into a miniature, forgotten, wind-scoured canyon. Once she would have known every shop, every office. On that corner there was once a butcher's shop; a line of pink neon pigs used to dance across its façade. In that building she had once gone every Tuesday afternoon for piano lessons, and now they are driving past the building where the lawyer's office still is; where at her mother's insistence, she signed a share of her inheritance away.

'Mum!'

'What is it?'

'It's red.'

'What's red?'

'The traffic light!'

'Shit.' The hit on the brakes flings them both forwards. Horns honk. Pedestrians stare, shaking their heads. On her palms a slick of sweat, which she rubs off onto the denim of her jeans. But she can do nothing about her heartbeat, pounding painfully in her upper chest, her neck. Rolling the window down, she gulps air.

'You swore,' the child says.

'Yes,' Sarah says. 'You're absolutely right. So I did.'

'You never swear.'

'It was an involuntary response,' Sarah says, thinking he must have been out of earshot pretty quickly the night he bit her. 'I thought we were going to crash.'

'But we didn't crash.'

'No. It was very close. But somehow we didn't crash.'

'What does invol... involun... that word you said mean?'

'It's not a swear word.'

'I know that.'

'Without meaning to,' Sarah says. 'It means, I didn't mean to do it. I didn't want to do it.'

36

As the weeks passed, Sarah began to feel the heat and light working on her. She remained resolutely pale compared with her co-workers and always covered up when she wasn't under cover. The fresh air and outdoor life brought changes of their own: a fine appetite, deep sleep and a kind of peace that she had not known since the long summer days of her earliest childhood, spent in the garden in the company of her father.

The professor, it turned out, was based in Athens and rarely visited. James, who was twenty-five, kept insisting that she'd learn more on the job than she ever would in a classroom. He convinced her that it was worth staying on for the European spring rather than hurrying back to late autumn in the southern hemisphere. In reality, she had no choice.

Her companions were a ragged bunch, friendly, hardworking, and they partied hard, too. One Swedish girl insisted that Sarah looked like her little sister and cuddled her quite ferociously when she drank too much vodka. As well as gleaning archaeological techniques, Sarah learnt how to say 'cheers' in over twenty languages. Most of the students came and went, staying for two weeks at a time; only she and James remained constant.

Patrick – all of that – was far away, hidden over the Earth's curve to the south of her. Here was life in the lulling warmth of sunny day after sunny day, swim after swim in a warm, tideless sea. When she thought of what she'd left behind, she saw it encased in ice, whipped round by cold Antarctic southerlies, all of it frozen and waiting for her return. In her heart she knew that it was only what still lay buried in the thyme-scented, limestone earth of Orua that remained untouched by time, yet she did not stir. She was not ready to return to the life she knew was really hers. There had been too much pain. Here, even while sifting soil day after day, she could rest and dream. She did not want to wake up yet.

At the end of three months, her visa ran out. James said he was returning to London. It was too hot to continue their work here; the dig would resume in September. He invited her to come with him, to spend a few months in England and find another job, visit the London office and get her airfare money refunded at last. It was her only option, but she knew when he asked her that it was what she'd been hoping for.

The screaming in her head had mostly ceased. This other feeling was new. Unsure what else to call it, she called it peace.

37

The motel is small and so close to the beach that they
can hear the sea through the open windows. Their
room is on the second floor and, as Sarah looks down
on the tops of the heads of the passers-by, the nausea
that has gripped her ever since they arrived in Port
Glass, that intensified so violently when she saw the
lawyer's office, surges through her again. Below her,
a few feet away, a woman who could be her mother
is walking by, handbag clamped under her arm,
sparse hair pulled over her crown. Dark glasses cover
her eyes, and as she watches the woman stumble,
Sarah thinks, *My mother is blind. Always has been.*
Alongside the sick feeling, a blade-sharp fear causes
seams of sweat to burst and trickle beneath her
clothes. Sarah squeezes her eyes closed, and when she
looks again, the woman has gone from sight.

The room is unbearably stuffy. There's no air left
in it. She pulls the collar of her shirt away from her
neck, fans her face with her hand. Why couldn't Patrick have chosen somewhere else to live? Why did
he have to come back here? Her instinct, the old

instinct, is to speed off, get as far away as she can as quickly as possible. *No,* she tells herself, *the time has come. You are not running away again.*

'Let's go out. We need to do some shopping.' Sarah stuffs some cash into her purse, checks that she has her sunglasses as well as sun cream and a hat for the child.

'Can we go to the beach?'

'If you like.'

The row of shops is sheltered by a deep veranda, protecting the shoppers from the summer heat, the winter rains. Outside, in the fresh gusts of sea wind, her breathing eases. They walk hand in hand, stopping first to look into the window of the bakery, where in the late afternoon all that remains are examples of fancily iced cakes designed to celebrate weddings, anniversaries, birthdays. They pass a sports shop, and a haberdashery with a display of teddy bears in ballroom dancing outfits, each bear couple frozen in some pose or embrace.

'Oh, look. What a great shop.' The child tugs her towards a narrow frontage. Behind a dusty pane of glass are dim vitrines packed full of stones: polished pebbles of garnet, splinters of amethyst, chunks of rose quartz.

'What a beautiful display of gemstones.'

'Can we go in?'

'Sure.' As they open the door, her gaze is caught by a black glass shard of obsidian, its edge lean and sharp enough to cut.

'Why do they call them gemstones?'

'It's from the Latin word *gemma*. It means bud or jewel.'

'A girl in my class has a friend who has a big sister called Gemma.'

'I knew a man who was called Jem. Spelt with a 'j' not a 'g' though.'

The child gives her his 'tell someone who cares' look and goes back to peering into the cabinets.

'May I buy this?' He opens his palm to show her a desert rose. 'For my collection.'

'Yes,' Sarah says, 'you've been pretty good, haven't you?'

'Yes, I have,' the child says firmly.

'You will not run away from me ever again, will you?'

'No, Mum.'

'Do you promise?'

'I promise.'

Sarah pays what seems hardly enough for the beautiful stone and the shop assistant wraps it in layers of white tissue paper.

38

It was a wet London Saturday not long before Christmas. The light and heat of Greece seemed decades distant, far longer in the past than a mere seven months. Sarah was walking down Long Acre when, unlikely as it seemed, she heard someone call her name.

'Sarah MacLeod? I thought it was you.'

'Mouse? What are you doing here?' His name was actually Martin and he had been a classmate of hers when she first met Patrick.

'I'm over here working for a bit. The usual OE. I guess you're doing the same.'

'Well, yes. I guess I am.' The finance office had said her funds should be reimbursed by Christmas and she had been saving hard, though it was more difficult here than in Greece, where nothing worked properly but everything was cheap.

'Let's grab a drink.' She'd been feeling tired lately, getting these losses of energy, usually in the afternoon. Most of her shopping was done. Ten to four, but around them it was growing dark already.

Sitting in Café Rouge, they drank coffee and then wine. 'I heard you'd gone to Greece,' Mouse said.

'I miss it.' Sarah turned her face to the window as if she might be able to look out and see the sparkling little beach, the sand the owner carefully raked each morning, the grapevines and the rows of peppers and of aubergines in his shady garden. She was even able to think with affection of his barbaric turkeys, whose aggressive antics and early morning shrieking she had described to James as menacing. There was little doubt in her mind that they were intelligent and knew their confinement was for no good purpose. Nothing had been the same since Greece. In England, life had got complicated again, not hers so much, but James's certainly. He was different here, less relaxed; more his real self, perhaps. She'd been feeling it was the right time for her to move on.

'Why didn't you get in touch with Patrick before you left?'

'But I did. At least, I tried to. I always seemed to get Kitty when I rang. I asked her to give him messages but I'm not sure now whether he ever got them.'

'That explains it, then.'

'I wrote and rang but it was hard. The place I was working in was so remote. And then they moved. I can't believe that Kitty didn't say.'

'Can't you?' Mouse smiled. 'She doesn't like me either. She doesn't like anyone who knew him before she did.'

'But you still manage to keep in touch with him?'

'He's got a part-time job so I call him at work. He knows what happens when I try and ring him at home. But in case you're wondering, he still loves her. In fact, they're engaged.'

'Oh,' Sarah said. 'I see.'

'What no one understands was why you just got up and left like that.'

It was true that she had not told anyone the real reasons. Nicki knew about Maria throwing the chair, of course. More recently she had told James. In fact, James had been less sympathetic than she expected, hinting that perhaps Sarah had overreacted. Patrick she would have told, if she could have. She felt certain he would understand. But it was too shameful to speak about to people who were no more than acquaintances.

'It's a long story. Perhaps you could give me Patrick's contact details. A work phone number would be great. And the home address as well. Why not?'

39

'Playground!' The child shouts. 'I can see a playground.'

'How does it look? Marks out of ten?'

'Eight, no nine. Definitely a nine.'

The pièce de résistance is a concrete whale, open-mouthed, its spout blocked by leaves, beached in a shallow, empty paddling pool. Sarah finds a bench, sheltered from the wind by a long, glossy stretch of escallonia. The child climbs and whizzes down the slide, swings back and forth, high then higher, light catching in his hair. At the top of the climbing frame he searches her out, makes sure she is watching him, before waving hugely. As Sarah waves back, she sees another child edge out of the shadows and shyly, cautiously, approach him.

Within a few minutes, the child and his new friend are playing 'It'.

'Mum's den,' the child roars, racing towards her and thumping against her side.

'12345678910 OUT OF DEN.'

The child bursts away from her, body arced to avoid the other child's reaching hands.

In her hand she holds the bag containing the desert rose. Another concretion, made from bladed gypsum, unlike the nearly smooth roundness of the boulders near Ariki. Without realising it, she has been squeezing it; now she feels a little bit of sand slip off its surface. She relaxes her grip, slides the stone into the safety of her bag.

When the child's friend has to leave, Sarah calls him. She strokes his hair and kisses the top of his head.

'Mum,' the child says, smiling. 'Get off.'

'It's time for us to go, too,' she says. 'Okay?'

'Okay.'

As they cross the road, Sarah feels the presence of the unseen sea ahead, the weight of the Southern Ocean ramped against the horizon. She tastes the salt of it on her lips; she hears its thump, a sound she has often mistaken for her own heartbeat. With a little yelp, without waiting for her, the child rushes down the dunes and out onto the sand. Sarah takes her time, keeping him in sight, looking back over her shoulder towards the town.

Sarah and the child begin to walk along the beach towards the headland, dunes on their left, sea on their right. The beach stretches for miles; the wind blows in from the sea, hard against their right shoulders. It drags the hair from Sarah's neck, blows it over her face, into her mouth and eyes.

The waves sound. The child stops frequently, bending to examine shells, stones, seaweed, driftwood, the light, white bones of birds placed on a wavering line of wind-sifted sand. Sarah hears the jingle of a harness, feels another pounding, the sound of approaching hooves. Blinkered horses run towards them, chained together. There is a racecourse on the flat land on the other side of the dunes.

Walking on this beach has always been good for thinking. It takes an hour and a half to walk from one end to the other. It is really two beaches, though where the boundary between them lies no one is sure. The waves are an icy, almost mint green; the white dunes are covered with strands of marram grass. The child zigzags and loops, running three times the distance as her; she wavers from a straight line only if absolutely necessary. When the child stops to avalanche a sand cornice into a tide pool, Sarah stops and helps him. The sand falls into the water, clouding it; she watches as it settles smoothly, as the water, momentarily agitated, unblurs, returning to translucency.

The sand is the colour of a dream, the colour of a new beginning, a colour so rare it seems unnatural. The child picks up handfuls of grains and stares intently at them, as if he, too, were trying to understand, before letting them fall through his fingers.

He begins to build a sandcastle, scraping lines into a mound with one half of a pale and flattish shell. The waves lift and sound, speaking in tongues. And then Sarah feels it. The ground is shaking.

It may be nothing more than the vibration of the waves filled with the weight of ocean. Perhaps it is only her, her too-fast-beating heart, as if she were still running from all these memories, not towards them as she promised she would.

'Let's sit down here for a moment, shall we?'

Sarah calls the child to her, just to be on the safe side, and watches him arrange shells while she waits for the shock to pass.

40

Sarah and Patrick had got back in touch and spoken tentatively at first, then more as they used to. It was the distance, of course.

'It was wrong of me to go away like that. Without explaining or saying a proper goodbye.'

'Sounds as though you tried to, and well, these things happen. It's all in the past now,' Patrick said.

'It's just so good to hear your voice.'

'Are you crying, Sarah?'

'Yes.'

'When we were growing up, you never used to cry.'

'Of course I did. Just never in front of you. Or anyone else if I could help it.'

'So what's brought about this sudden change?'

'Oh, it's not sudden. It's been going on for months. I've only just discovered why. It's the baby. It's already started changing me.'

'You're pregnant? Oh my God. I must admit that's the last thing I ever imagined you'd say.'

'Thanks.'

'I don't mean it like that. I'm just a bit shocked, that's all.'

'Imagine how I feel.'

'Listen, Sarah. Come on. You're a fighter. You'll be a great mum.'

'I sincerely doubt it. I'm not even twenty.' When she thought about it, she tried not to use the word 'disaster'. That's what James had said. In shock when she found out, she made an appointment to end it but had not been able to go through with it. James said he understood, that he'd do the right thing by her, but most of the time she felt worried and occasionally very, very scared. All her plans had changed, again. She would not be going home, not yet.

After the child was born, she got in touch with a lawyer in New Zealand. The main reason was to change her will so that she could leave her share of the house in Orua to her son. A week or so later the lawyer rang her. There was a serious problem concerning her inheritance. Her mother and sister had been borrowing money against the house in the mountains, taking out ever larger amounts over the years. Now their debts ran to hundreds of thousands of dollars. Interest-only repayments. Over two-thirds of the equity had been drained from the property, and Nicki and Maria were in arrears with their monthly payments.

'This is bad,' the lawyer said. 'And there's also a further loan in the form of a caveat. They didn't tell you?'

'No. How could Maria and Nicki take out these loans without involving me?'

'The bank isn't actually obliged to inform you if two of the joint owners take out loans like this. It's not best practice but neither is it illegal. Try and agree with your family what to do, and if you can't you'll have to take action.'

'But she's my mother. How could she lie to me like this? How could she do this to me?'

'You signed a mortgage agreement?'

'When I was eighteen. For three thousand dollars. Maria swore to me it was to buy a new car. Nothing more.'

'The loan was repaid,' the lawyer explained, 'but the mortgage stayed on the title of the property. That's how they got the subsequent loans.'

When the lawyer sent copies of the loan documents through, attached to an email, Sarah printed them off. There, in black ink, her sister's and mother's signatures one, two, three, four times down the margin of every page. Everything laid out before her, in plain and simple English. The documents spread over the desk so that they covered every surface. The baby asleep on her lap, Sarah dialled her mother's number. She had written to Maria telling her that she was pregnant, giving her contact details in London but had heard nothing back. As she listened to the ring tone, the slight arrhythmic delay caused by vast distance, her heart tumbled over and over, as if it had washed loose of her body and was caught in a never-quite-breaking wave.

'Hello?'

'Mum, it's Sarah.'

'Sarah? Well, what have you got to say for yourself?'

'Listen, Mum. Just listen to me for a moment, will you?'

'What is it?'

'I've been rewriting my will and when I sent the documents to my lawyer he told me that you and Nicki had taken out loans on the house in Orua. For hundreds of thousands of dollars. And now the account is in arrears.'

'There aren't any loans.' The voice, still as recognisably her mother's as the signatures were, was now toneless, cold.

'I've got the documents in front of me. Copies of the loan agreements you signed. From the bank.'

'The bank is lying. There aren't any loans. We paid them back.'

'There are over four hundred thousand dollars in loans. Current loans. Which have not been paid back.'

'They're lying.'

'They're not the ones who are lying.'

'How dare you accuse me of lying! I worked every day after your father died to pay for everything.'

'The original loan for three thousand dollars was paid off. The one you said was for a new car. These are new loans. I've got the papers here. They're covered in your signature. And Nicki's.'

A pause. And then Maria said, 'I've got to go.'

'Why won't you speak to me about this?'

'I've got to go.'

'I'm your own daughter, and you won't talk to me. Why have you done this?' Betrayed me. Stolen what Dad gave me. Left me responsible for your debts. 'You've never even got in touch to ask about your grandson. For God's sake, tell me why!'

Sarah waited but Maria said nothing. Silence. But there was something in the silence. Sarah felt it, a message as lifeless as the darkness through which it had travelled. The silence settled coldly in her chest. Maria had wanted to hurt her; Maria had succeeded in hurting her; Maria was pleased with what she had done.

And then it was the beginning of September again, and James was due to return to the dig in Greece. Sarah asked him not to go, unsure how she would cope alone, but he went anyway. She had begun to take legal action, and the process was complex, expensive and slow. The child was a poor sleeper; most of the time Sarah was too tired to think.

After James left, she found herself ringing Patrick, who listened and sympathised. In James's absence, he gave her advice about how to act and deal with the complex legal fallout which resulted from Maria and Nicki's deception. Patrick even intervened on her behalf, trying to reason with Maria and Nicki, but he failed as she had done, as the lawyer who was acting for her had also failed. The money she had saved was burnt up by the necessary fees.

'When are you coming home?' Patrick would always say, before they said goodbye. 'Isn't it about time you came home?'

He listened to her make excuses. James was not here. They were spending all their spare money on a lawyer to fight the legal battle. The child needed this and that. The roof was leaking, again. The car needed to be repaired.

Really, it was more than that. The love between her and James had melted away and only remained, embodied, in the bawling, bustling, dazzling, smiling bundle of energy that was their child. After James's dig season ended, she couldn't be sure he'd be living with them again.

41

She has been so lost in thought that she has forgotten to check her watch. There is only one place left to visit before they see Patrick, the place that Sarah has been dreading, perhaps most of all. But she must go there. And she must go before she sees Patrick. She recognises it is necessary, and he does as well.

Since she arrived in Port Glass, she has felt as if the blood were draining out of her, leaving her hollow, empty. But the walk has restored her, the sea smell, the sand, the sight of the waves; she feels calm as if, taking the place of her absent blood, the cold green ocean is inside her, its strange energy now powering her. Last night, through the uncurtained window, she saw the moon, nearing full, rise above the sea, and watched as it darkened into something more substantial, a chalky, shadowed whiteness as the sky around it blackened. Looking at the moon's bright face, Sarah thought, *I have travelled to a place that you cannot buy a ticket to; there is no train that goes there, no boat, no plane; there is no map that you can follow to find it; there is no road. It lies on the other side of that circle of light. It is always dark there, and it is always cold.*

On the top of the dunes, the marram grass, the toitois, bend in the wind. As she holds the child's hand, pulling him up the slope, their feet slip so that the cold, damp grains below the surface spill over their bare feet, and then slide off again, leaving a trail of holes in the sand behind them.

'Where are we going now?'

'I lost track of time. It will take us too long to walk back along the beach. Let's get a bus back to the motel.'

'Are we going to see your friend?'

'Yes. One more stop and then we'll see him. Quick, stick your hand out.'

'Why?'

'So the bus sees us and stops.'

'Why has the bus got those big hooks along the front of it?'

'They used to hang prams and pushchairs on the hooks. Years ago. When I was a little girl.'

'With the baby in?'

'No.' Sarah smiles. 'The baby sat inside with the mummy.'

It is unexpectedly warm in the bus; in the artificial climate behind the glass, there is no wind to strip the heat from them. The child takes her hand. As Sarah leans her head against the window, and stares out at the familiar lines of trees, it is as if she is eleven years old again. She is walking up the road from Nana's house. At home, the neighbours have come in and are cleaning, vacuuming the echoing rooms, taking the curtains down, bundling up bedding. The windows are open to let in the warm, early autumn air, and Maria is crying and saying, *What's going to happen to us? What are we going to do now? What are we going to do?*

'Did you say something, Mum?'

'No, darling. Was I mumbling?'

'Yes. Yes, you were.'

'Sorry. I'm a bit tired. I didn't sleep so well last night.'

'I know. I heard you.'

'Heard me?'

'Writing in that book. The one with the golden crown on the cover.' The child makes looping movements with his hand. 'Why do you always write in pencil?'

'Because I like the sound it makes on the paper.'

The child mimics it. '*Wish, wish, wish.*' And then, tipping his head back, he yawns mightily.

'Did the sea air make you tired?'

'No. You?'

Stretching her arms above her head, Sarah yawns as well. 'No, I'm not tired at all.'

After letting them off outside the motel, the bus pulls away from the kerb. As Sarah unlocks the car and opens the door, securing the child in his seat, the cooling breeze from the sea at her back, she thinks, *Sometimes it's just a matter of waiting; waiting for history and memory to align, like stars over a mountain, and lead you home.*

Along the straight road, they drive towards a headland, an arrow's flight from Patrick and Sarah's old school. The headland has been there waiting, the backdrop to their play, the endless hitting, kicking, chasing of balls, that time that was somehow everything, that has held all the moments since within it.

'Look, Mum.'

Something is coming out of the sea – a penguin, small and weary. It stumps across the sand on its way to the safety of the cemetery cliff. No dogs are allowed here. This is the place where all those years ago Sarah and Patrick and hordes of other children from their school planted hundreds of flax bushes, creating the penguins' first sanctuary. She has been worried about what she'll say to Patrick. But she must tell him this: that whatever else happens, whatever they decide to do now, they once did something that has mattered; they once did something that has made a difference.

As they walk along the beach, Sarah picks up a shell the soft pink-umber colour of cameo, with a heart that twists in on itself. She knows what its heart looks like because the shell has been broken open; she has never found this type of shell intact. A set of stairs climbs the side of the headland. Sarah and the child clamber up it. At the top is another cemetery, another much more recent grave.

I'm sorry, Sarah thinks as she puts the broken shell down on the headstone. *I should have tried harder. I should have accepted it… I wish that I had told you… I wish that…*

But there she must stop, because she still does not know what she should have said or what she should have done.

I'll try to… I promise that… that I'll do what I can for him. I can't say what will happen. No one can, can they?

'Did many cats die in the earthquake?' the child asks.

'Kitty wasn't actually a cat. She was a woman Mummy knew. A friend of Mummy's. You see here. Her real name was Katherine.'

'Oh. Why does it say *Wife of Patrick* on there?' the child asks.

'Patrick was Kitty's husband.'

'Your friend, Patrick? The one we're going to see?'

'Yes, that's him. You were named after him and my grandfather. Your great-grandfather. Remember I told you about him? On the way over. When we were in Singapore.'

'Singapore?'

'We've been to so many places, haven't we? It gets confusing, doesn't it?'

'It's very windy here,' the child says. 'My ears hurt.'

'My ears hurt, too. Shall we go?'

'Goodbye, Kitty,' the child says.

The guilt she feels about Kitty almost stopped her from coming; now she is glad that it didn't. Next to her shell is a bunch of late summer flowers, so fresh that they might have been placed there only hours before.

Her journey is almost over. She has shared the only inheritance she has left, a handful of places, a few stories, with her young son. He can remember or forget them as he pleases. All she has left to give to him is what remains of her time and her attention.

When the child was born, the induced labour came crashingly fast. She could not have any pain relief other than gas and air because the baby's heartbeat was distressed. At times, the pain was so bad that she blacked out. The room was full of medical staff expecting the worst. But then he was delivered, too weak and shocked even to cry. For all these years and now, when she looks at the child, feels his hand in hers, she has only one hope: that she will always feel about him what she felt when he first came to her and she returned from the darkness to meet him.

42

And then one day the telephone rang and it was Nicki, furiously angry.

'Listen, Sarah. I've an offer to make you.' She named a ridiculously low sum, and said she'd buy Sarah's share in the house in Orua before the bank's auction.

'You must be joking.'

'It's more than you'll get if we have to go through with this fire sale.'

'And who's responsible for that? Why did you and Maria do it? What did you even spend all that money on?'

'There are always more things to spend money on. Oh, for God's sake, you always were a little stuck-up prig. And you still are. You haven't got a clue.'

'Doesn't it mean anything to you? Dad left it to both of us. It was the one good thing we had, and you and Maria had to go and destroy it. Imagine how Dad would feel if he knew. It's our last link with him. With what he wanted.'

'What do you mean, Dad this and Dad that. He only left it to us to spite Maria. He wasn't even your father, you idiot. You must know that.'

What Nicki said haunted Sarah; she turned it over in her mind with no way of knowing whether or not it was true. If not Ross, then who? Jem? And if Ross was not her father, then why leave half of the house to her? Her mother knew the truth, but no one else knew Maria's thoughts, the secrets that lay curled in her heart of hearts. Only her actions spoke so loudly that eventually Sarah could no longer ignore them. With painful clarity, she knew then that she should have listened to her instincts that day in the lawyer's office and lost then the love her mother never had for her.

Sometimes, sleepless in the London dark, the house in Orua seemed almost visible before her, the blue lines on that thin, translucent architect's paper rose up before her eyes again, that map into the future which Ross had laid out for them: carport, dining area, kitchen, living room, atrium, hallway, bedroom one, bedroom two, bathroom, WC, laundry room, and there, at the end, an odd shape in the corner, Sarah's room. She remembered seeing it, hers the only name written on any of the spaces.

It tormented her at times: the house as a ship, rocked on waves; the house as a symbol of their failure to love one another, to remain a family after

Ross's death. She'd studied enough to know that houses and fences and buildings of all kinds were just there to give people a sense of stability, safety, control, when really there was none to be had. It was much harder to do what Ross had done – build a new home for them all, knowing that time, his greatest gift, was running out. The future was not his, but theirs, and this is what they had done with it.

Through circumstance, carelessness or intent – it hardly mattered – Sarah's shared past with her family lay shattered around her. The devastation caused by her mother and sister had severed all ties between them. Finally, she was free of them.

She was free.

43

Sarah had just dropped the child at school and was driving back to the flat when she heard the news on the radio.

Hours earlier, during the local rush hour, a massive earthquake had struck Bishopstown, where Patrick and Kitty had been living for some years. At home, Sarah switched on *News 24* and picked up the phone. She rang every number she had for Patrick – his mobile, his work number, his home phone – but he did not pick up. She sat at her computer all day and then all night, sending email after email into the darkness.

That was the moment she realised. That after all of this time, after everything that had happened to them both, that despite living on the other side of the world from him, she loved Patrick. She had loved Patrick from the first day she met him.

It was more than likely that she would always love Patrick, even though he had chosen Kitty, even though he might never be hers.

44

'Whose house is this?' The child asks.

'It's Patrick's house.' The house of his childhood to which he has returned. A wisteria grows over the veranda. It is a typical Victorian villa, of a kind she has been in many times before. Inside she knows she will find a long, dark central corridor with rooms opening out on either side of it. At the front is a sun porch filled with aged geraniums, a wooden front door with a stained glass panel, patterned with a design of running waves, a worn brass knocker in the shape of a penguin. 'Do you like it?'

'It's nice.'

'Isn't it?'

'Are we going inside?'

'Yes.'

'How long for?'

'I'm not sure. We're going to stay here for dinner. We could well be quite a while.'

'Will there be toys?'

'I don't know. Do you want to bring your bag of Lego in, just in case?'

'Okay.'

'Wait a minute, love. Before we go inside. Can you listen to me for a moment?'

'Yes.'

'Remember we talked about the earthquake? About how lots of people were hurt?'

'I remember.'

'Patrick was there when it happened. He was hurt. And he was upset. Very, very upset. But the main thing you'll notice is the way he looks.'

'I don't know what he looks like.'

'Well, what you'll notice, when we go in, is that part of one of his arms is missing.'

'Oh. But I can play with my Lego?'

'Yes.'

'And we can go in now?'

'Yes.' Sarah opens the door. 'Let's go in.'

Notes and Acknowledgements

All my love and thanks to Adam, Iris and Lauren for their unfailing support and encouragement during the long years it took to write this book.

Special thanks to Clio Gray for her invaluable advice and guidance. Thanks also to Gregory Heath, Marilyn Denbigh, Rupert Wallis and Penelope Todd for their comments, and Literature Works and Arts Council England for a full manuscript Free Read. My gratitude to the New Zealand Society of Authors and Creative New Zealand for the excellent support they have given my writing.

This book was written with the support of the Mentor Programme run by the New Zealand Society of Authors (PEN NZ Inc) Te Puni Kaitahu O Aotearoa and sponsored by Creative New Zealand.

My sincere thanks to Louise Boland and everyone at Fairlight Books.

The title was inspired by an unpublished fragment of writing by Robin Hyde quoted in *The Book of Nadath* (Michelle Leggott, ed: Auckland University Press, 1999): '... *who travels with his dream travels with a dark torch.*'

FAIRLIGHT MODERNS

Bookclub and writers' circle notes for all the
Fairlight Moderns can be found at
www.fairlightmoderns.com

SOPHIE VAN LLEWYN

Bottled Goods

When Alina's brother-in-law defects to the West, she and her husband become persons of interest to the secret services, causing both of their careers to come grinding to a halt. As the strain takes its toll on their marriage, Alina turns to her aunt for help – the wife of a communist leader, and a secret practitioner of the old folk ways.

Set in 1970s communist Romania, this novella-in-flash draws upon magic realism to weave a tale of everyday troubles that can't be put down.

'It is a story to savour, to smile at, to rage against and to weep over.'
    - Zoe Gilbert, author of *FOLK*

'Sophie van Llewyn has brought light into an era which cast a long shadow.'
    - Joanna Campbell, author of
        Tying Down the Lion

SARA MARCHANT

The Driveway Has Two Sides

On an East Coast island, full of tall pine moaning with sea gusts, Delilah moves into a cottage by the shore. The locals gossip as they watch her clean, black hair tied back in a white rubber band. They don't like it when she plants a garden out front – orange-red *Carpinus caroliniana* and silvery blue hosta. Very unusual, they whisper. Across the driveway lives a man who never goes out. Delilah knows he's watching her and she likes the look of him, but perhaps life's too complicated already...

'This devourable novella is one part Barbara Pym, one part Patricia Highsmith and all parts Sara Marchant.'
— Jill Alexander Essbaum, author
of *Hausfrau*

KAREN B. GOLIGHTLY

There Are Things I Know

Eight-year-old Pepper sees the world a little differently from most people. One day, during a school field trip, he is kidnapped by a stranger and driven to rural Arkansas. The man who calls himself 'Uncle Dan' claims that Pepper's mother has died and they are to live together from now on – but Pepper isn't convinced.

He's always found it hard to figure out when people are lying, but he's absolutely certain his mother is alive, and he's going to find her...

'Pepper proves a tenacious, resourceful hero.
Immensely readable and sweetly told.'
- Marti Leimbach, bestselling author of *Daniel Isn't Talking*

ANTHONY FERNER

Inside the Bone Box

"As he tiptoed his way through the twisting paths
of sulci and fissures and ventricles, he'd play
Bach, something austere yet dynamic."

Nicholas Anderton is a highly respected neurosurgeon at the top of his field. But behind the successful façade all is not well. Tormented by a toxic marriage, and haunted by past mistakes, Anderton has been eating to forget. His wife, meanwhile, has turned to drink.

There are sniggers behind closed doors – how can a surgeon be fat, they whisper; when mistakes are made and his old adversary Nash steps in to take advantage Anderton knows things are coming to a head...

Anthony Ferner is a former professor of international business and is published widely in non-fiction in his field. He has one other published novella, *Winegarden*.